# The Perfect Proposal

## By Regina Andrews

Writers Exchange E-Publishing
http://www.writers-exchange.com

The Perfect Proposal
Copyright 2014, 2015, 2019, 2020, 2025 Regina Andrews
Writers Exchange -Publishing
PO Box 372
ATHERTON QLD 4883

Cover Art by: Sandy Cummins

Published by Writers Exchange E-Publishing
http://www.writers-exchange.com

# Contents

# Dedication

For my parents with love and appreciation for their timeless example of love. To my husband Jonathan for everything. With very special thanks to Sandy Cummins of WEE publishing for her superlative editing skills and unfailing support, and to Karen Wiesner for her cover art design and encouragement.

# Chapter 1

Taking a deep breath, Lindsay Richardson tightened her grip on the thick leather handle of her father's briefcase, trying to draw some of his strength and fortitude from it.

Something warned her she was going to need all of that, plus a special prayer, to face her first day of work at Copley Industries. She opened the door to her boss's office for their initial meeting.

"I said no interruptions, Claire, please." She heard a man's voice coming from the other side of the cavernous office. He spoke without looking up from his desk as he shuffled through a stack of papers.

"I'm sorry. I'm not Claire. But she told me--"

"Claire doesn't run Copley Industries. I do. That's the First Commandment here."

Lindsay cringed at his use of that particular phrase, but she bit her lip and gripped the leather handle of the briefcase even tighter than before.

He stood up and switched on the recessed copper-rimmed lights. Now Lindsay could see him clearly. She was in trouble. She had walked into the wrong office.

"I'm sorry for intruding, I have an appointment with Mr. Copley, but it must be your father, not you. I didn't open the right door."

His clear blue eyes narrowed. From the tip of his sandy hair to his designer shoes, everything about the thirty-something executive spelled *advantage* to Lindsay. She felt like an alien life form under his intense scrutiny.

"I'm your Mr. Copley. For now," he said, coming toward her from behind his desk. There was something in his tone of voice Lindsay didn't understand. "Call me Dean."

Lindsay felt like a bobble-headed doll as she nodded. "Okay."

"Who are you, anyway?"

"I'm Lindsay Richardson, from St. Gregory's Elementary School."

When there was no response from him, she continued talking really fast, before he could tell her to leave. "We saw each other on Saturday. I was handing out leaflets about the church music group at the apartment complex. You're an owner there, and so's my sister. Don't you remember?"

"No. What did I say?"

"You mentioned something about my timing being bad."

"One might say it's still true." He raised one eyebrow.

Lindsay grew more flustered than before. "You told me it was private property and..."

"'We don't allow solicitations on this premises' Right. Now I remember. You are Meg's sister. I see the resemblance." His eyes swept over her in a quick, experienced appraisal. "Except you looked more comfortable in those sweatpants."

Lindsay almost died from embarrassment. She hoped he wouldn't notice the deep flush she felt racing across her cheeks.

"But why are you here now?"

"After you went in the house, your father came by. We talked for a few minutes and then he offered me a job here. He told me to show up Monday, so here I am. I've already done all the paperwork with Claire, and I thought I'd be meeting with him when I came in here."

"Well, he didn't tell me. How do you like that." He gave a laugh.

Lindsay had to keep thinking quickly, before he decided he didn't need her around. "I guess he figured I'd explain it all to you, then. Like I just did." Concern crept into her heart. What if he didn't keep her? She needed this job. "I'll be going."

"Where's my cell phone? I just had it."

She followed him over to his desk, laden with files and magazines.

He pressed a button on his telephone. "Claire. Where's my material about Lindsay Richardson?"

"You don't have any, Mr. Copley," Dean's secretary explained in a patient tone of voice from the other end of the speaker. "She brought all her materials with her." He disconnected the speaker, and imitated her: "She brought all her materials with her."

He sounded just like Claire. Lindsay wanted to laugh at his antics, but was stopped by his intense stare. Then he smiled, and Lindsay felt the charge of 550 volts of electricity course through her.

He walked past his desk to a putting green, complete with waterfall, set along the windows in the far corner of the office. Picking up a golf club and focusing on his putt, he mumbled: "Second commandment: never work with a close personal friend. And my dad; I can't believe he hired you and didn't even tell me. What's your job?"

"I'm the new Assistant Executive Secretary."

"I don't need one. Why'd he hire you?"

"He knew my father," she answered quietly. "They were very close friends, they went way back. In Africa during the war, and all. So I guess, when he learned about my father's..."

"Oh, just missed." With a groan, Dean tossed his putter aside.

She gripped the leather handles of her father's briefcase even tighter. *Give me strength, Lord.* She didn't want talk about losing her father with Dean. The pain was too fresh. And he didn't seem too concerned about her, anyway. He appeared to be very wrapped up with his own agenda.

Dean slapped his palm against his forehead. "You know, he always does this to me."

"What?"

"Tells me I'm running the company and then just does whatever he wants, anyway. Sometimes I really wonder why I'm here." He plunked into a chair.

"I know how you feel," she couldn't help saying. "I'm sort of wondering that, too."

He looked at her curiously, as if seeing her for the very first time.

Locking into his bright blue stare, Lindsay felt herself starting to get pulled into his world. And like a swimmer competing against the current, she struggled to stay afloat.

A moment passed before he spoke again. "You'd better be able to multitask, to work for me."

"After caring for my mother, who has Alzheimer's? No problem."

"And always be straight with me. I can't stomach a liar."

"I don't know any other way to be." The plush, rust-colored carpet she stood on felt like it was turning into quicksand. How could she keep her focus with him staring at her like that?

Taking another deep breath, she asked: "Doesn't your father work here?"

"Not really. I run Copley Investments, our subsidiary investment firm. My father started Copley Industries as Copley Air, making the units that heat and cool buildings all over the world. He's semi-retired now, allegedly. But actually, his main pastime seems to be making my life tough and undermining my authority."

With her own father gone for not three months yet, it hurt Lindsay deeply to hear him speak this way about his own father.

"If that's the way you feel, then why don't you say something to him about it? That would be honest." She spoke from her heart. At that moment, his power over her future meant little to her, compared to how she felt about her father.

Dean stood up and walked closer to her. She felt his energy as he approached. And, like the maple trees thrashing against the

November gales blustering outside, she held her own and stayed rooted firmly to her spot.

"You're seriously telling me what's honest? Really? Well, Lindsay Richardson, I have the perfect proposal for you."

Lindsay hoped he couldn't hear her heart thumping in her chest.

He continued: "Why don't you let me deal with my father in my own way, and why don't you go find your office."

"All right. Thank you, Dean." She reached out to shake his hand but he dismissed her with a nod towards the door. He wouldn't shake her hand. How humiliating!

As she walked away, she could feel his eyes on her back. She primly smoothed her navy blue skirt and gave the dark bun coiled at the nape of her neck an efficient pat.

Then she straightened up on purpose, just to show him that Lindsay Richardson had a real backbone--even though their meeting had been iffy.

"Ask Claire for 206," she heard him call as she closed the copper doors behind her.

Even though she was just starting a new job, why did the latching of the doors sound decisively, and eloquently, final to her? Gripping her father's briefcase, she repeated one of her favorite prayers: "As one door closes, another one opens."

Alone in his office, Dean twirled in his leather executive chair, ideas and impressions swirling through his mind. This new, surprise hire, Lindsay Richardson looked nice enough. And she had "it": a closeness to her family he longed for but could never grasp. He could tell from the look in her eye, especially when she spoke about her father. He had tried not to let on, but he could tell she hurt. But how could he make her experience at Copley Industries a long and happy one? If he did, he would just be playing into his father's hand.

*She really looks like she needs the job, though. How can I fire her on her first day? I can't. I won't.* Dean shook his head, glancing at the framed photo of his father on one side of his desk. Of course he'd make it work for Lindsay. His issues with his father weren't her fault.

Somehow it seemed like his dad was always there. As a youngster growing up, not a day went by without his father asking him about his activities. All through his formative years, his father had been a stern and steely presence. And Dean still felt his influence, even to this day. Yet, it might have been nice to sometimes feel he could speak to him, one on one, without having to defend himself. Without the steel.

Of course he appreciated all his father had done for their whole family. Gratitude was the only reason that he had gone into the family business. He was certainly not suited for it. And his heart wasn't in it, never had been.

Ronald, the golden boy, was the one who should have been sitting in this chair, not him.

His friend Gordon had to hear about this latest outrage. He reached for the phone. As he did, Dean looked at the hideous scars spread across both of his hands, aching physical reminders of the pain he had been through the day he had accidentally killed Ronald. He knew Lindsay had been embarrassed when he rebuffed her extended hand. A simple gesture of gratitude on her part, a handshake, was impossible for him. The scars on his hands made shaking hands out of the question for him. The pain from his past was a pain he was still feeling to this very day.

The helicopter crash had occurred years ago. But when would the pain ever go away?

Suite 206 was in the corner of the old brick manufacturing plant, so typical of the turn-of-the-century industrial complexes lining Providence's Blackstone River Valley. The Copley family had completed a total renovation five years earlier, creating an exciting, state of the art office and retail facility to house the design, manufacture, and distribution of their primary business, Copley Air.

Lindsay could remember her father mentioning its much-touted opening when it had been publicized in the newspapers and on television at the time, since it provided such a boost to the local and regional economy.

She looked around admiringly. The original exposed piping and ductwork was now painted cherry red. Additions and structural changes over the years had resulted in an odd-angled lay out throughout the whole place.

It dawned on her that the odd design of the place duplicated the odd path her life seemed to be on right now. Five years earlier, when the building had been completed, it never would have occurred to her that she'd be working here. Yet, as life would have it, here she was.

"Good morning, again," said Claire, with a friendly smile. The plump blonde bustled over to her, silver bracelets jangling. "How's it going so far?"

"It's had its twists and turns," Lindsay replied.

Claire gave a crooked smile. "With Dean, I'm not surprised. Do you know what projects you'll be working on?"

Shaking her head, Lindsay answered: "We haven't gotten that far yet."

"Well, there's plenty of time for that later. But if you like to travel, there are a lot of opportunities here. Anyway, I brought you a nice hot cup of tea." She handed Lindsay a china cup and saucer. "How do you like your office?"

"I've never seen anything like this in my life," she said.

"It is unusual," Claire agreed. "Just like Dean."

Lindsay thought she detected a note of motherly pride in Claire's pleasant voice. As far as she was concerned, to call him "unusual" was a bit of an understatement.

Wandering towards her work alcove, she admired the smoked-glass shelves mounted on the wall by copper brackets near her desk, filled with assorted hard-covered books and plants. The lower shelf was loaded with various copper frames, and each frame had different people in it.

"I see the Copleys love copper, Claire, because it's so close to their name. But who are all these people? Does Dean have a big family?"

"I don't know who they are, Lindsay," Claire answered. For the first time, the bubbly secretary seemed subdued. "They came with the frames."

"You mean nobody knows any of these people?" Lindsay hadn't ever heard of anything like that. "They're just decoration?"

"It's more than that. Ever since the accident, he doesn't allow any of us to keep any personal pictures anywhere. It's one of the few rules here. He has one picture of his father on his desk, that's it."

Lindsay was confused, and asked: "What accident, Claire?"

There were tears in Claire's blue eyes as she answered.

"The helicopter crash, twelve years ago. You're probably too young to remember." She dabbed her eyes.

"I think I remember something about it," Lindsay said slowly. "It didn't happen around here, though, did it?"

Claire shook her head. "No. It was in Vail, Colorado."

"I remember now," Lindsay's expression was somber. "Not everyone made it."

Claire nodded sadly. "Dean was piloting the chopper that went down. They lost his brother, Ronald...the shining star of the family. My husband, Normand...and...others. Dean still has the scars on his hands from the fire..."

Before she could finish, Dean came into the office.

"Where's my file on the Wyman project, Claire? Please," he added. The strong lines of his chin and jaw were tight.

Lindsay stepped aside to let him in, and as she did, Dean walked straight into her path. He collided with Lindsay so forcefully that the cup and saucer in her hand went flying, spilling hot tea all over the front of his suit.

"Oh no," she said. "Oh, I'm so sorry!"

Dean shook his head impatiently but didn't say anything. He just grabbed for his handkerchief.

"How clumsy of me. I'm such a klutz!" Lindsay continued, snatching the handkerchief from him. When she did, she noticed his hands...and the scars, just as Claire had told her. The red, thick skin was rippled and warped along the top of both hands, up beyond his wrists. That must be why he didn't shake hands, she thought.

She could only wonder what it must have been like to know he had caused his brother's death. How had he recovered? He must have incredible fortitude... Could he possibly have a strong faith to have such fortitude?

"This shouldn't be too much of a problem," she chattered, hoping he hadn't noticed her looking at his scars. "Club soda and sea salt are very effective on tea stains, believe me, I've had to..."

Dean made a face and took her hands firmly in his own. "That's quite enough, Miss Richardson," he said.

Mortified, humiliated and certain that she was about to be fired, she froze in mid-dab. "I'm really sorry. I don't know what happened."

"It was an accident." Dean's lips were thin and his voice was flat. "We all know that accidents can happen."

Lindsay knew his words were filled with meaning, for he had been though a terrible accident. What a deep man he might be. She puffed her cheeks out in a grateful sigh of relief. She noticed that his eyes seemed to soften.

In that moment, with his features relaxed, he looked so fresh and natural. Lindsay couldn't help but notice how genuinely handsome he was. It was as if he was freed from all the artifice and his real self was shining through--if only for an instant. She opened her lips to

# Chapter 2

"But don't you have a social secretary for that? It doesn't sound like what someone in my capacity would be doing." Her eyes searched his face for some clue as to the direction she was to take.

"Call it what you want. I'm not one for semantics. I'm one for results." His voice left no room for discussion.

"Understood. I just don't want to step on anyone's toes." Lindsay moistened her lips.

"Instead of worrying about stepping on someone's toes, why don't you do your job, before you're stepping out the door? And as far as your 'capacity' here, Miss Richardson, I think that's ultimately up to me." Dean turned on his heels and quickly left the area.

Lindsay tried to calm the rhythm of her pounding heart. All she knew was her first order of business was to get Dean a date for the gala that night. Then a thought struck her like a bolt of lightening and she dialed her home number.

"Hello?"

"Meg, it's Lindsay. Look, I need a huge favor." She could just picture her sister's wide-eyed amazement as she heard her request. As chairman of the Modern Language Department at Blackstone University, her many duties left her little time for socializing with the likes of Dean Singleton Copley.

A few moments later, she went into Dean's office and found him tapping a pencil on his desk to a blaring Amy Grant CD.

"Well," she announced, "I found someone to fill in, even though it is very last minute."

"Like who?"

"My sister, Meg. As you know, our dad was on the Board of Directors for the Heart Association. I called her and she'll be honored to represent his memory by attending the gala with you."

Meg's mouth formed an "o" in astonishment when she saw Lindsay in her black velvet party dress. "You look so beautiful, Lindsay. Daddy would be so proud."

Lindsay's eyes filled with tears. "Don't get me started, Meg. We don't have time for these floodgates to open. Besides, you owe me big."

"I can't help it if I have the stomach flu," Meg wailed. She pointed to Lindsay's cell phone. "Leave that on in case I need you."

"I'll be sure to call and check in." Lindsay finished putting on some soft pink lipstick. She hoped her mother would have a peaceful night. Unfortunately, sometimes, without warning, she would become confused or frightened, as she had the night before. And Meg wasn't as used to it as Lindsay was, which worried her to no end.

"Here he is, here he is; go get the door." Meg sounded more like a teen than a forty-something university professor.

"Meg, get a grip? This is not a date. I'm only doing this for my job security at Copley Industries." They had enough to worry about, and money was right up there with all the things they didn't seem to have enough of these days.

She said a quick prayer as she stood at the door. It wasn't easy for her to reveal her private life to someone who seemed so detached and worldly, but she was determined to try. "Come on in," she said to Dean.

Up went his eyebrows. "I thought Meg was coming."

"It's me." Lindsay tried to act casual, but her heart was pounding like a jackhammer. "Meg has the stomach flu. Come in, please? I don't want my mother to get cold."

"Right." He walked into the kitchen, filling it with the warmth and quiet strength that only a man could offer.

And that whiff she caught of his cologne...so warm and woodsy...and so very masculine. Remembering her father, she felt a pang of loss that she tried to brush away. There was too much going on around her to get carried away in wishing Daddy was still with them.

"Nice to meet you, Meg," Dean said "Sorry you're not feeling well enough to come tonight. How do you do, Mrs. Richardson?"

"Hi!" Mrs. Richardson called, reaching out her arms to him.

"She likes you," Lindsay said.

Dean placed a brightly wrapped gift box on the table.

"What's that?" Lindsay asked.

"It's for all of you." Dean smiled. "Open it," he urged.

"All right."

They all watched as Lindsay carefully removed the lovely paper and placed the bright, shiny bow to one side.

"Oh, it's beautiful." She took the gift out of the box to reveal a lovely snow globe depicting a traditional nativity scene.

"Hope you all like it," Dean said.

Lindsay found the transformation in Dean to be stunning. He seemed like a different man than the one she had met earlier that day. Turning the key under the snow globe, strains of "Away in a Manger" filtered through the kitchen.

There was almost something magical in the atmosphere in the room as they listened to the music. Lindsay glanced at Dean, wondering how he was doing. From her experience, most people felt uncomfortable and ill-at-ease around Alzheimer's patients. But Dean seemed perfectly relaxed.

Then she turned to her mother, who gazed at the snow globe, nodding her head to the beat of the music. Alzheimer's patients frequently responded very positively to music. It had a calm and soothing effect. "The healing power of music," Lindsay murmured when it ended.

Dean smiled at Mrs. Richardson. "Early Christmas gift. Good night, now."

Mrs. Richardson looked up at him and smiled, clapping her hands. Dean took her hands gently in his own. Lindsay wondered if his scars would frighten her. But Mrs. Richardson didn't seem to notice them at all. She smiled and everything was fine.

Lindsay and Dean stepped into the crisp evening, stars dazzling overhead.

He started his luxury car and Lindsay fastened her seat belt. Smooth jazz filtered from the CD player, calming her frazzled nerves. She turned to wave at Meg, framed in the kitchen window.

"Are you all right, Lindsay? You're breathing kind of fast."

"I must admit I'm a little nervous. Since my father died, I've hardly left my mother's side. It's hard for me to leave her in someone else's care, but I'm trying. That's why working is such a big step for me. And going out is really unusual for me and I'm not so sure how comfortable I am about it." A thought struck her. "In fact, I'm thinking that maybe I should take my own car. That way if something happens and I have to get home quickly, I can just bolt."

"There's no need to worry about that. If you need to go, I'll get you home. It'll give me a chance to escape all the nonsense." He gave her a glance.

"That's thoughtful of you." She looked over at him, pondering his words. For the first time, she noticed how sharp he looked in his formal wear.

"Anyway," he continued, "I'm bolting as soon as I can, so be ready to go when I say so. Believe me, you'll be home early."

"Fine," she said, stifling a yawn.

"Bored with my company already?" The corners of his mouth edged upwards.

Lindsay was appalled and embarrassed. "Oh no, not at all. I'm so sorry. I wish it were that simple." She sighed. "You could never in a million years guess why I'm so tired."

"Try me."

"My mother got very disoriented last night. I don't know how much you know about Alzheimer's..."

"Not too much, but I know it's terribly difficult for everyone."

She nodded. "Sometimes patients get confused. And last night, my poor mother was scared out of her wits. Insisting that Meg and I had stolen her stuff and that she had never been in her bedroom before. She's lived there since 1968."

Dean let out a slow whistle. "Oh boy. Has this happened before?"

"Never to this extent. It got worse and worse as the night went on. Meg and I had all we could do to calm her down. Unfortunately, from what I've read about Alzheimer's, this means she's probably getting into a worse phase of the disease."

"I'm sorry to hear that." Dean negotiated the car skillfully around one of Barringtown's tree-lined curves. "So who's going to be with your mother during the day now that you're working?"

"That's a tough one. Meg has classes, committee meetings, student advising and endless office hours as Department Chairman. She will try, but most of the time we'll take my mother to the Senior Center. She loves people."

Dean was silent a moment before he spoke. "You have a nice family, Lindsay. I can only hope things go all right for you."

"Thanks, Dean." Lindsay said a silent prayer of agreement in her heart. *Me too, Lord.*

A few minutes later, Dean pulled into the circular, terra-cotta entryway of the beautiful Providence Eastmont Hotel, and handed the car keys to the valet.

Landscaped terraces, brilliantly illuminated for dramatic effect, and cascading exterior waterfalls added to the excitement and glamour that filled the bustling activity in the entryway.

Lindsay stepped out of the car, amazed at the number of people already surrounding them, all clamoring for Dean's attention. There was so much tumult and activity around her, she could barely hear herself think.

"Here, take my arm."

"I'm fine, thanks," she replied, even though it was a struggle for her to keep her balance in the three-inch heels she had dug out from the back of her closet. It occurred to her that since she had met Dean, it had been a struggle to keep her balance. *That's where you come in, Lord, I'm counting on you to lift me up and keep me on a steady, even keel.*

Dean reached out and gripped her elbow, tucking her hand securely into the crook of his arm. "There, isn't that better?" The smooth material of his formal wear felt nice against her bare arms.

"I like to think I'm just fine on my own."

"That's quite obvious, Miss Richardson."

Was he making fun of her? She looked at him, trying to see any signs of sarcasm. But he just looked at her and smiled. Suddenly, a flash bulb popped out right in front of her, blinding her temporarily.

Dean spoke in a firm tone. "Mike Malloy, roving photographer. If I didn't know any better, I'd think you were stalking me."

"Just doing my job. The Register has me after you, Dean, 'cause anything about you sells papers." The photographer matter-of factly snapped his bubble gum.

"Then my next venture will be buying The Register, so I can give you a better assignment."

"Please do. But first make sure I get a raise." The scruffy photographer hurried off into the well-dressed crowd.

The look on Dean's face as he watched Mike disappear made Lindsay wonder what he was really thinking. He was so hard to read.

They navigated through the automatic doors towards the elegant lobby. Lindsay wondered if she needed to check in at home, then decided to wait.

A beautifully attired woman approached them. "Darling, so good to see you." Waving her jeweled hands, she hastened towards Dean, accompanied by a dangerously thin young woman of about twenty-five years old.

Lindsay immediately recognized the older woman as Dean's mother, Mrs. Blaire Astor Copley. She was often featured in the newspaper for one of her numerous charity benefits. Photographed probably, Lindsay surmised, by Mike. She smiled at the thought.

"Hi Mom, hi Kathy," Dean smiled back at them.

The show of affection between Dean and his mother warmed Lindsay's heart. Mrs. Copley's blonde hair was swept up into a fashionable French twist, and her coral evening dress glittered magnificently. Together, they lit up the lobby.

"Dean, where's Gwynneth?" Mrs. Copley asked.

"She couldn't make it. That's why Lindsay filled in at the last minute. I'd like you both to meet Lindsay Richardson, my new assistant."

The two women turned simultaneously towards Lindsay, who felt their gazes were as bright as Mike's flashbulbs.

"Hello, Lindsay." The smile Lindsay saw plastered on Mrs. Copley's face did not seem to come from her heart. Her eyes remained steely cold.

"I'm very pleased to meet you, Mrs. Copley."

Although Mrs. Copley's expression was gracious and pleasant, the tilt of her head told Lindsay that she was on the receiving end of a merciless once-over.

"And I'm Kathy, Dean's sister," the emaciated girl extended a lily-white hand, which contrasted garishly with her sequined, midnight blue gown.

Lindsay knew she was out of her league with these two society women, but she managed to accept Kathy's handshake with a smile. "Nice to meet you."

To Lindsay, the two women seemed to be from another stratosphere. A caregiver, she had once read, always feels set apart. And yet, she hadn't felt set apart earlier in the day when she met Claire...or Dean, for that matter, either. Nervous, but not different.

"Where's Dad?" Dean asked, scanning the room.

Mrs. Copley gave a dramatic sigh. "In the back with the hotel staff, making sure everything is perfect. You know him." She rolled her eyes.

"We'll see him soon," Dean told Lindsay.

"I hope so," she answered. "It would be nice to see him again."

Kathy flipped her raven hair dramatically over her bare shoulders then glanced at her wristwatch. "We've got to run, Mummy. We're supposed to meet the Tiptons now because we missed them today at Alvaro's."

Lindsay recognized the name of Alvaro's as the most expensive jewelry store in the state, and the Tiptons as one of the state's most prominent families, with Mr. Tipton a former Attorney General.

"Duty calls," Mrs. Copley laughed theatrically, tilting her head back and exposing a long graceful throat. She wiggled her impeccably manicured fingers in the air, saying: "They promised they found me a beautiful estate piece that will flatter these hands to death. See you inside. Dean, I hope you practiced your speech. And try not to keep Daphne waiting too long. After all you are the star attraction." Off they breezed across the lobby, towards the main entrance of the ballroom.

Lindsay was combating the onset of a pounding headache. "Who's Daphne?" she managed to ask, purely out of politeness. Suddenly, she felt very tired. And she wanted to check in at home.

"Nobody, really. She belongs to the Club."

"Oh," Lindsay murmured, "the Club."

"Yeah, the Ivy Club. Up at the University."

"I've heard of that."

"I think Dad wanted your father to join." Dean guided her across the plum-colored carpeting towards the center of the lobby.

She nodded. "And they had his surprise retirement party there." How her heart ached for her father.

He stopped them under a huge crystal chandelier, twinkling merrily in the festive night.

"In we go," Dean said. "Remember, we're not staying long."

Lindsay nodded. "Just like the Romans entering the Coliseum to be sacrificed."

"What a thought, Lindsay."

"I'm out of my league here, Dean. We both know it."

Dean looked at her, and Lindsay thought she saw kindness in his eyes. "There's no one here in your league, Lindsay. Remember that."

Lindsay's eyes nearly popped with surprise from the unexpected compliment. "Thank you." She saw him nod in acknowledgement as they walked through the ballroom.

The atmosphere was crackling with excitement. A string quartet played background music for the guests as they entered.

"I know those musicians," Lindsay said. "They're college students from my church."

"We've had them here to play for us in the past, they're very good."

"They really are. My father helped line them up." She smiled at Dean. "I can feel him here."

Dean nodded, but didn't say anything. She wondered if she was imagining things - was he looking at her a little longer than necessary?

She admired the beautiful, extravagant decorations. Tiny white lights glittered in neatly clipped topiaries, boxwoods and oranges, intertwined with fragrant stargazer lilies. A quick tally gave her a total of nearly fifty tables. "There must be over five hundred people here."

Dean nodded. "It's our biggest fund raiser all year, and we're so fortunate to have members of the Minutemen attending this year."

"The Minutemen football players? I would have brought my camera, I'm such a big fan."

"Don't worry, I can always call your friend Mike back if you want some pictures. He has a thing for you." Dean smiled and gave her arm a squeeze.

"No, I'm too small-time, Dean. How do we find our seats?"

"We're over here." He nodded towards the dais.

Lindsay's eyes widened in surprise. Wait until she told Meg what she had missed! She followed him through the crowd, paying careful attention not to trip on the hem of her dress or to catch her heel on one of the long salmon pink linen tablecloths. Lindsay heard a voice behind them.

"Dean, Dean? Is that you?"

She tugged on Dean's arm. "There's someone calling you."

As Dean turned around, Lindsay turned with him and found herself face to face with Gwynneth Holt. Perfect skin, perfect hair, perfect dress...she was simply Walking Perfection.

"I can't believe it. You said you couldn't come tonight." Dean seemed surprised to see her there.

"I had a last-minute change in plans." Gwynneth's sapphire blue eyes glistened.

"I'd like to introduce you to my new assistant, Lindsay Richardson. She filled in for you."

"At the last-last minute, Gwynneth. Nice to see you." Lindsay extended her hand, but Gwynneth ignored the gesture.

Did she have scars, too? Lindsay took a quick look. Nope, Gwynneth's hands were lily white. *Oh well.* "Look," she said, "you're both here now. Dean, why don't you go ahead and I'll just get a taxi home. It's no big deal. I don't mind."

She tried to move away, but Dean wouldn't loosen his grip on her elbow. She shot him a look, but he just ignored her.

Instead, he continued: "You know, Gwynneth, my mother and Kathy will be glad to see you, too. And looking so well."

Gwynneth smiled for the first time. "Do you like my dress?" She twirled, pewter chiffon floating all around her statuesque frame.

"Yes, very nice," Lindsay chimed in. Someone called "Gwynneth", and when she heard her name, she was gone in a flash.

Dean's eyes warmed when he looked at Lindsay. "I spend all my time trying to escape those claws. My mother thinks we are destined to be together."

"But you don't?"

"No, I don't. I don't know how to get the message into their heads without hurting them, either. They don't want to listen to me, or hear what I have to say."

"Maybe it'll just take time," Lindsay shrugged.

They took their seats on the dais and Lindsay sent a text message to Meg at home. When she read her sister's answer "All OK" she sighed a prayer of relief.

"How's everything at home?" Dean asked. She could feel the warmth of his arm next to hers and she tried to ignore how good it felt to her, how comforting.

"So far, so good."

"Glad to hear it."

"I love this salad with gorgonzola and walnuts." She swallowed. "It seems to be a fill-time position to deal with all these different personalities, Dean."

"I'm accustomed to it, Lindsay. I've grown up with it all around me. Sometimes I think it's more a part of me that I realize or even want to admit."

"But why, though?"

Dean shrugged. "Little melodramas are a part of my whole social context. They mean nothing. After a while, the truth doesn't even seem that different from a fib."

Lindsay could only wonder what it would be like to have her life become so obscured and so complicated that she could't see the truth. "I can see what's happened with you," she answered. "But I think you're on top of things. It isn't like you have to get things on track. It's how you feel inside."

❧ ❧ ❧

Meg was waiting for Lindsay when she came back into the house.

Lindsay took a deep breath. "Things are nice and calm here, Meg. And the house smells like gingerbread."

"We managed. Thanks for messaging. How was it?" Meg asked, eyes bright with excitement. "It sounds like just the sort of evening I would have loved." Meg's blood boiled, thinking of the night she had missed.

"Nice." Lindsay shrugged off her coat. "But not my scene at all. I'm glad it was only one night." She gave her mother a big kiss.

"Deborah called. She couldn't believe it when I told her where you were."

"How's she doing? I can just picture her out on her patio overlooking those beautiful cactus-covered valleys of Phoenix. I'll have to call her tonight and tell her everything."

"That's what best friends are for." She smiled. "And sisters. Where's my 'thank you', little sis?"

Lindsay gave Meg a big hug then sat down at the kitchen table.

"Any chance you'll be doing it again?" Meg asked after a pause. "Or that I'll get a chance to fill in for you again soon?"

"I hope not, Meg. I like having this job and everything, but I'm not really interested in making a career of being a stand-in for Gwynneth Holt--who was there after all!"

Meg was astonished when Lindsay told her the juicy details of the night. She was delighted that Lindsay had enjoyed her night out, but worried about her well-being with everything so shaky at home.

As she listened to Lindsay, Meg wondered how to tell her--or if she should tell her--that things at the house that night hadn't been peaceful at all. Things were changing in the Richardson household, and Meg just hoped that her little sister Lindsay was ready for all the challenges ahead.

# Chapter 3

Dean was up earlier than usual the following morning. Gray and drizzle again, all day. Probably turning to snow. Typical November. Made it special fun to go out for his morning run.

The hustle and bustle of College Hill hadn't really started yet. He pounded along the broad, tree-lined boulevard that intersected the city. With his breath coming out in billowing clouds of dragon steam, he ran as if his very life was at stake.

What was it about Lindsay Richardson that made him feel as if everything he had made himself out to be was a complete fraud? And, even still, why didn't that bother him? In the past when anyone had shaken his sense of self, he had found a way to avoid them and keep them out of his life. But when he thought of Lindsay, his heart felt good.

He certainly had good reason to, he thought, turning in to the city Botanical Gardens. But he had to be careful not to get too close. The winding path seemed to mirror his turning and twisting thoughts. She represented his father's ultimate control over him, because just by being employed at Copley Industries by his father it proved he wasn't really in control. A control he had spent the past twelve years trying to overcome. Break free from.

Or had he? His pace quickened as the truth chased after him. There was one possibility too tough for him to ignore. But there it was, staring at him, confronting him at every turn.

Perhaps he really didn't resent his father at all. That would explain a lot of things. Maybe, just maybe, he didn't feel as if his father had much control over him at all, either. Perhaps he just had been telling himself that as a defense mechanism against finding out who he really was, and admitting that he alone was responsible for his own course in life.

And more, maybe he liked to be near his father, to work with him. To try and operate as a family, despite how dismal their prospects for the future were without Ronald. Dean liked carrying on in spite of everything.

Could his resentment be a way of actually staying close to his father? A way of masking his unease at losing his father, too?

He reached the banks of the Blackstone River, noting a flock of Canadian geese in majestic formation above. Maybe he, too, could rise above some things. He would have to think about it. Maybe he already had, and didn't even realize it until now. A small smile curved across his face.

*I'd better be careful that no one finds out*, he thought to himself. *Or they'll all think I'm going soft.*

Which didn't really seem like such a bad thing.

Frozen rain greeted Lindsay when her alarm went off the following morning. She took a moment to collect her thoughts before the day began. Had last night really happened? Had she really attended the Heart Association gala with New England's most eligible bachelor?

Most women would be in raptures about being with Dean, but to her it was much more. Oh yes, she had enjoyed being with Dean--probably a little bit more than she wanted to admit. But what she had really loved about last night was the fact that she had been able to represent her father, even though it was in a very low-key way, which perfectly matched his low-key style. And despite not having a chance to speak with Mr. Copley Sr., being there had made her feel closer to her father.

She couldn't help but wonder, though, about the Lord's plan for her. He had placed her smack dab in front of a human tornado! It seemed the ones who could answer her questions weren't around these days to help her figure it all out.

The snooze alarm buzzed and Lindsay dragged herself out of bed and peeked in on her mother. For the time being she was sleeping peacefully. Then she peered in on Meg, who was also still sound asleep.

For the moment, peace. She headed down the hall to the kitchen and put the water on for the morning coffee.

One hour later, she was seated in her office when Claire came in, breathless.

"Here's today's paper," She tossed the edition of The Register onto Lindsay's desk. "You two are the newest hot couple here in Rhode Island."

"Oh no," Lindsay groaned. "How did this happen?"

"I don't know. I wasn't there," Claire replied with a shrug. "But I do know that this is the kind of thing that happens whenever Dean Singleton Copley is around."

"I can't believe this." Lindsay was horrified as she read the society column headline. 'Copley Melts for Commoner'. "What will my church think?"

Claire shrugged. "They should have more to do than gossip about you, Lindsay, don't you imagine?"

"I guess so," Lindsay agreed. "But I'm concerned this might really bug them."

"Whatever." Claire remained impassive and indifferent. "I'm going to get our coffee."

"Thanks, Claire," she called after her new friend.

After she called Meg to check in on her mother, she decided to set up her filing system. When would she find out what her duties would be? And she couldn't help but wonder what Dean would be like this morning when she saw him.

Would he be as cut and dry and as businesslike as yesterday? Would he allow the professional veneer he put forth to be a bit more transparent than he had earlier? Lindsay thought about all he had told her about his father, all she had seen with him and his family...and how naturally he had melded with her mother and family...

A knock at the door interrupted her thoughts.

"Come in," she called, putting down her apple muffin and dabbing the crumbs from her mouth.

Her mouth dropped open when Claire came into the office--carrying a baby that appeared to be about eight-months old.

"How adorable, Claire," Lindsay jumped up. "What's this little doll's name?" She met the warm little dimpled hand that reached for hers. The baby quickly grabbed Lindsay's index finger and gurgled.

"Cassidy," Claire replied. Lindsay noted that her tone seemed subdued.

"Cassidy Copley?"

Claire shook her head no. "Cassidy is my daughter Belinda's baby--and my first grand baby."

Why was she a little relieved to know the baby wasn't Dean's? Then, Lindsay couldn't believe that Claire was a grandmother! She was just about to say so when Dean burst into the office.

"What have we here?"

For some reason, Cassidy began crying and screaming.

"Ssshhh!" Lindsay frowned at him. But then she couldn't help but smile.

He smiled back at her, all fresh-faced with his hair tousled from the windy November morning. Lindsay's heart lurched when she saw him, so vibrant, so vigorous, with his radiant good health and body...he was so *alive*.

He beamed at her, then turned to Claire and stretched out his strong arms to the little girl in her embrace.

"The littlest angel! My best employee! Come to Dean-o-dyno!"

Cassidy giggled and reached for him. He cradled her gently and started humming "I Left My Heart in San Francisco" as Cassidy looked at him adoringly, patting his face with one of her dimpled hands.

"This is a nice surprise," Dean said, waltzing in place with her in his arms.

"I couldn't find someone to take care of her this morning," Claire explained. "Is it okay if I watch her here while I work, Dean?"

"No problem," Dean said. "It's good therapy for us. Boosts our morale." He looked at Lindsay. "One of my pet projects is starting an onsite day care center. Maybe that's what I'll put you on, Miss Richardson."

"I'd like that." As she looked at Claire and Dean with Cassidy, a thought struck her.

"You both look so happy and natural with children. Why don't you come with me to Good Book Buddies at lunch time? We can go and be back in an hour."

Dean gave her a glazed look but didn't say anything. Claire asked: "What's that, Lindsay?"

"It's a reading ministry at my church. One afternoon a week, on our lunch hour during the work day, we go into the schools and read with a child. It gives them one-on-one attention."

"Oh, never," Dean sounded insistent. "You'll see a blue moon in the midday sky before you see me do that." He handed the baby to Claire. Lindsay wondered why he sounded so different about this than he was when he mentioned the day care center. Could it be the church part, perhaps?

"I will," Claire said. "What day do you go?"

"Actually, it's today. If that's all right with you, Dean. The church is right around the corner."

Dean answered quickly. "I don't have a problem with sponsoring it through my company. But I will not get involved personally."

His tone left no room for discussion. But Lindsay wondered how he would know so quickly that he didn't want to get involved?

"What time do we leave?" Claire shifted Cassidy to her other hip.

"Twelve-thirty, and like I said, we'll be back in an hour sharp."

"Fine. I'll have Helen in Credit watch Cassidy until we get back."

She closed the door quietly as she left.

"That is one beautiful baby," Lindsay commented.

Dean nodded thoughtfully. "That she is."

"Why don't you come along with us to Book Buddies, Dean? You might like it."

As soon as she spoke, Lindsay sensed a wall had gone up between them.

"You're involved in a lot of activities, it seems, Lindsay. It's nice that you like children. But I'm wondering what qualifies you for this job, anyway? My father just made up this position for you, basically, so I didn't review your resume."

Lindsay didn't miss the challenge in his voice or the glint in his eyes. And it made her wonder where he was coming from, to act this way. He had been so nice with Cassidy! Maybe DSC needed a little TLC. She jumped at the chance to share some kindness with him and to prove herself.

"Between my music ministry and my experience in the Diocesan Office of Communications I have the experience to deal with the challenges of this position."

"And how does St. Gregory's fit in?"

"Like I mentioned, I was the music teacher there for the past six years."

Dean frowned; two worry lines forming in his brow. "And?"

"When my father passed away unexpectedly at the end of August, I asked them for a leave of absence," she continued.

"You were that upset?"

"It wasn't for me. It was only until I could be sure that my mother was okay."

After a pause, Dean asked: "Then what?"

"And, the only person they could find at the last minute like that wanted a full-time commitment or nothing at all. So they let me go. They almost had to."

"Nice," he said, his tone bitter.

"I was mad at first, too, Dean. But there's always a reason for everything." She shrugged. "Then I saw your father, and he found out I'm between gigs, so to speak."

Shaking his head, Dean scoffed. "I never could have been that philosophical in your shoes, Lindsay. You seem pretty casual. I would have raised the roof to save my job. Just out of loyalty, you know, to myself and to my employer, too."

"I understand that protectiveness better than you can imagine. For six years my job was everything to me." But there was another aspect to the situation that put everything into perspective, an aspect over which she had prayed long and hard. After reflection, she discerned what was truly important in the situation, and it had turned out to be much bigger than herself.

"But do you think that you would have done so at your mother's expense, Dean? It really came down to that. However, even though I've worked in Communications, I wasn't at all prepared for this."

She indicated the copy of The Register on her desk, their color picture splashed across the front page.

Dean glanced at the paper. "Oh, that. It's par for the course. You look great, by the way. You're very photogenic," he said. "It doesn't bother you, does it?"

"Yes, very much." Lindsay couldn't believe it, but she thought that Dean seemed genuinely puzzled. She continued: "It looks like we're an item."

"So what?"

Exasperated, Lindsay answered: "It's embarrassing. I'm not a socialite. I'm Lindsay Richardson. And I never try to make myself out as something I'm not. My parents taught me to live that way and I firmly believe in it."

"Nice speech."

"I mean it. You might not feel like that, but I do. I'm not used to this."

"I know. I'm sorry you're so upset and embarrassed."

He rested against the edge of her desk, arms folded across his chest.

"Doesn't it bother you?" Lindsay really wanted to know.

He shrugged. "I'm used to it."

"Well I don't know how you stand it. I would never get used to it!"

His eyes held hers. "Then maybe you're not Copley Industries material."

"Maybe I'm not," she blurted. "But I think I am. I want to be, if you'll give me a real chance."

Just then her phone rang. *Why didn't I set my voice mailbox up first?* She could have kicked herself.

"You'll have to give that some thought," he advised. "But in the meantime, let me make it up to you. Lunch is on me today."

"But Good Books Buddies is today..."

Dean raised his hand in a gesture of 'halt'.

"Just this once, it's okay for you to extend your lunch hour. Work first, then those kids." He grinned. "Well, me first. Now you'd better answer your phone."

No sooner had he left the room than Lindsay grabbed the receiver.

"Hello?"

"Lindsay, it's Mike." Mike Malloy's voice came through the phone loud and clear and brazen, just like him.

"I'm not thrilled with you, Mike. Thanks for humiliating me in front of the whole state."

"Now, now, that's a great picture of you. You should be thanking me."

"Well I'm not." Lindsay counted to ten silently to calm herself. "All of Rhode Island thinks I'm after the great Mr. Copley."

"I gotta sell those papers to keep the circulation up. Pays my bills, you know."

"Mike, did you just call to hear me thank you for the picture? Or was it just to remind me to set up my voice mailbox?" She unwrapped the cellophane from her new desk calendar.

His hearty laugh nearly filled the room. She held the receiver away from her ear.

"No. Lindsay. I called to ask you out to dinner."

Lindsay rolled her eyes. "Thank you, anyway, Mike. But I'm not a socialite. And I'm busy for the next three years.."

"Can't say that I don't take a hint. All right. I'll try back again in a few days."

Lindsay frowned as she hung up the phone.

The rest of the morning flew by in a blur. She set up an appointment with one of the company's design engineers to discuss a site for the center. She also set up a spreadsheet for the day care center in her files, and met with the secretarial pool. When she returned to her office from a tour of the facility, she realized it was time for lunch. Some delicious aromas greeted her as she walked to her door.

"Hmmmm...smells wonderful, Claire. Chinese?"

Claire had a mysterious look on her face. "Not me," she answered vaguely.

Lindsay wondered what was going on. When she opened the door, she found out, though. There sat Dean Singleton Copley in her office, surrounded by a buffet of Chinese lunch items.

"What's this?"

"The welcome lunch I planned for you, but now I've turned it into a lunch to smooth over your outraged morals. I'm sorry you were embarrassed." That famous Copley charisma, so often written about in the media, filled the room. "Some dim sum?"

Putting her oversized shoulder bag down on the leather love seat, Lindsay crossed her arms and frowned.

"How can I resist? It's an executive order. But to be honest, I just lost my appetite."

"Oh, lighten up."

She took the plate he offered her. "Real china?"

"Copley Industries is a world-class operation. We don't do disposables. White or fried?"

"I'd rather do it myself, please." She watched as he ignored her and served her white rice before heaping his own dish with fried.

"Shrimp?"

"Chicken."

He served her first, then loaded up on the spicy Szechwan shrimp.

"Egg roll?"

"Mixed vegetables." She admired the brightly colored vegetables as they covered her rice.

Dean placed three egg rolls on his own plate. "I'm seeing a pattern here."

"I saw it before you did."

"Tea?"

She shook her head. "Soda. See?"

They sat at a table on one side of Lindsay's office with a beautiful view of the Blackstone River.

"This is delicious."

"Claire helped me," Dean answered. "She doesn't want you to leave."

"I've only been here one day. I'm not a quitter."

"That's good to hear. Just try not to be too sensitive."

"I'll try."

"It is and it isn't," he answered. "I didn't get a chance to ask you yesterday how your father knew my dad."

Lindsay moistened her lips. Memories of her father always put her in a state of emotional overload.

"I thought I already told you. They knew each other from the war."

"Really?"

Lindsay wondered how he could not know about this. "They served in Africa together. Your father was a pilot and mine served as a mechanic. After the war, they kept in touch. My father went into the Administration of the Postal Service, as Director of Personnel."

"Human Resources these days," he interjected wryly.

"And your father started all this." She waved her hand.

"It started as Copley Air," Dean said proudly.

"Then they were on the board of the Heart Association together, for years." She eyed him quizzically. All the years Dean had been working with his father, and he had never talked about Edward Richardson to him? It seemed odd to her. "I'm surprised he never mentioned it to you."

Dean nodded thoughtfully, and then a wry smile slowly curved his full lips. "You might have noticed, Lindsay. There's a lot of things that my father neglects to mention to me."

She felt as if the air between them was charged with atomic particles. "I guess there's a lot of different ways you can be close to people," she said. But from her point of view it was inconceivable that close people wouldn't share endless details, like the Richardsons did.

"I never said we were close," he answered. Did she detect a note of regret in his voice?

There was a silence between them in the room, a vast span Lindsay had no idea how to bridge. She wrestled against the little tug of sympathy for him that was nudging at her heart. *Go away*, she scolded...but it only persisted in needling her all the more.

A soft knock, which Lindsay recognized as Claire's, interrupted them. She poked her head in.

"Dean, Sam Burchfield is here. He says it's almost 12:15 so make it now and forget the three o'clock." She raised her eyebrows.

"I've got to meet him. There goes lunch, but it was nice while it lasted." He shook his head.

"Yes, it was, thank you." She said politely.

"Don't forget, we have a planning meeting tomorrow at the State House," he called as he left the room.

"Who's he talking to?" Lindsay asked, turning to Claire.

"You!"

Lindsay raised her eyebrows. "Me?"

"You have to go to the meetings with him," Claire explained. She and Lindsay piled up the dishes. "I'll call catering for the rest of this."

"This was so nice, Claire. Thank you." Lindsay was truly touched. "I guess it's an understatement to say that Dean is overextended."

Claire smiled. "I don't know how he does it all."

"Well, being a type A personality, an overachiever, and a really good multi-tasker give him a good head start."

Laughing good-naturedly, Claire agreed: "I guess you're right."

They got their coats and headed to the parking lot. On the way down, Lindsay had an idea.

"Say what, Claire, I just had a thought."

Claire looked at her expectantly.

"How about if you see if you like my church and then give some thought to helping us out with our holiday penny social. We could sure use your organizational skills. And your charm."

"Oh, you're good, Lindsay."

Claire hoped her shyness wasn't showing in her blush. Flattery had always worked on her before, but Lindsay had no way of knowing. She told herself at fifty, she was too old for flattery...but inside, she thought getting involved in another project might be the best thing in the world for her. Belinda was always busy, and Cassidy was growing so fast. Worst of all, it was all too true that her dear husband Normand would never be coming back to her. It was time for her to live her own life.

"I'll think about it." And with a brave smile, she drove off with Lindsay to the church. From what she had seen thus far this morning, Lindsay Richardson was going to turn out to be a really good addition to the Copley Industries team.

# Chapter 4

Lindsay dressed with special care the next morning, choosing a cream-colored pants suit, brown leather boots, and a paisley scarf. She wanted to be at least presentable, because she had the planning meeting to attend with Dean at the State House that day. And just in case Mike was there...she wanted to be sure any pictures of her did not reflect poorly on her family or her church. Or, of course, her new position at Copley Industries.

Her ringing phone interrupted her thoughts. That phone sure rang a lot for someone who had just started here.

"Hello?"

"Lindsay, it's Meg."

"I missed you this morning, Meg! How are you doing?"

"I'm fine, and so's Mom. But you won't believe the delivery we just received from Providence Gourmet!"

"Really? That's such a nice shop." Lindsay recognized the name as one of the state's most prestigious specialty gift shops.

"I know. It's beautiful." Meg glanced at the items covering the kitchen table. She smiled at her mother who smiled back at her.

"There's a beautiful hydrangea, a rose bush and two amaryllis in ceramic planters, plus a gourmet treat tray with fresh fruit, cheese and crackers, and truffles."

Lindsay couldn't believe her ears. "Who sent it?"

"I'll read you the card."

Lindsay could hear Meg rustling the envelope. "To the Richardson family, with caring and friendship. It's signed DSC."

"Dean sent it?" Lindsay was amazed.

"I guess so. What doe this mean, little sister?" Meg's voice sounded playful.

"Don't even go there, Meg! Thanks for calling. See you around five."

❧ ❧ ❧

"Okay." Meg rang off, and, turning to her mother, placed the rose bush in front of her. "Now, doesn't that smell nice?"

Meg kept up a constant stream of chatter to keep her mother engaged.

"Now, you wait here," she said after giving Mrs. Richardson her morning pills. "I'll be back in a jiffy." Mrs. Richardson seemed docile and calm, and gave Meg a sweet smile.

Dashing down the hall to the bathroom, Meg held her breath that her mother would be okay. One of her biggest worries was leaving her mother unattended, even briefly.

"I'm right here with you," she called, hoping being all alone in the kitchen would not frighten her mother.

After a moment, she hustled back down the hall.

"There, that didn't take too long," Meg said, stepping into the harvest-gold kitchen.

But the cold blast from the wide-open back door was all that greeted her.

⁂

"Snow showers." Lindsay glanced out the window as she passed Claire's desk on the way to Dean's office.

She would exercise her self-control, and say a polite 'thank you'. But inside she was wondering if he thought they were a charity case. Hopefully not.

"Fast-moving cold front," Claire said in reply, not looking up from her keyboard.

"Is Dean in his office?"

Preoccupied, Claire nodded. "Uh-huh."

Lindsay knocked on the oversized copper doors to Dean's office before she walked in.

"Dean, I just wanted to speak with you about the daycare."

She stopped in her tracks when she saw Dean and Gwynneth on the love seat, their heads bent close together, deep in conversation.

"Oh excuse me." Through her shock, Lindsay saw Dean smile while Gwynneth threw her a look.

"Come on in, Lindsay, I was just going to call you in." Dean was as suave as ever, not missing a beat.

"Oh no, that's okay. I'll catch up with you shortly. Hi, Gwynneth."

Gwyneth rolled her eyes but remained silent, her expresso-colored suede pants suit showcasing her long legs.

"Gwyneth will be working with you on the onsite day care center," Dean said. "You guys can get going on it."

"We'll meet in my office," Gwynneth said.

"Great. Just let me know when." Heart pounding double-time, Lindsay closed the doors quickly, wishing the floor could open up and swallow her whole.

Her proud little heart had no place in the world of the Copleys and the Holts.

But wait a minute. What was Gwynneth going to be doing on site from now on? What were she and Dean really discussing so intimately? And why was Gwynneth getting an office? She took a deep breath. *All that is really none of my concern, Lord. Thank you for this job and please guide me in Your ways.*

She checked her watch. Almost time for the State House meeting. She wondered if Dean would want to go with her or meet her here. She was applying some clear lip-gloss when Claire came rushing in.

"Lindsay, I have your sister Meg on line two. There's an emergency at home!"

*This can't be happening,* Lindsay thought as she pulled into her driveway. Neither her mother nor Meg were anywhere in sight.

Panicked, she raced into the living room. Maybe they were already back in the house and this nightmare was over. No Mom. No Meg. She flew back into the dining room. Nothing.

"Mom?" Lindsay called. "Mom? Where are you?"

An oil truck raced around the corner of the sleepy neighborhood's street. The sound of the engine drew Lindsay to the door.

"Mom! Meg!" she called. She opened the door fully and ran back out into the driveway, shivering more from anxiety than from the cold. A harsh wind blew snowflakes chaotically around her, mirroring the tumult in her head.

"Mom?" she cried.

*Where was everyone? The neighbors? Had an ambulance already come and gone?*

She reached the edge of the driveway. Turning to her left, then her right she looked across at the neighbors' wide lawns. Each incline, each patch of ice loomed threateningly before her.

Where could they be? Lindsay knew how men and women with Alzheimer's would often wander away from their houses. Some were miraculously found and returned home safely. But others weren't so lucky.

"Please, God, let them be all right." Her voice nearly echoed in the bleak and deserted neighborhood. Lindsay fought back the tears that were stinging her eyes. "She's already suffered so much."

She hurried down to the edge of the street, no knowing which way to turn. Then she heard it, faintly at first.

"Ed?"

Her mother's voice was gente, ladylike, almost playful, as she called for her deceased husband. The poignancy of it nearly broke Lindsay's heart. But she forced herself to hold it together.

"Ed, darling?"

Spinning around to find which way the sound was coming from; she spotted her mother walking toward the street from one of the neighbor's back yards.

Relief flooded through Lindsay as Meg, too, came into view.

"Mom," Lindsay called gently, "I'm here."

She walked across the snow-blanketed grass, trying to look calm and nonchalant so she wouldn't scare her mother. Inside, her heart was beating double-time. The past few moments had seemed like a lifetime.

Her mother gave her a saintly smile. "Hello! Aren't you nice!" It was as if she were greeting a stranger. Lindsay noticed the snowflakes in her hair. Hopefully, she wouldn't develop pneumonia from this episode.

"Come on," Lindsay held out her hand, "you like me and I like you." She knew that a soothing tone would matter more to her mother the actual words she was using.

"Of course," Mrs. Richardson said, extending one of her beautiful hands.

Lindsay rubbed her mother's hands vigorously, trying to warm her up. Her shivering mother seemed chilled to the bone.

"There we go, Mom," she said comfortingly as she led her back to the house. Out of the corner of her eye, she saw Meg wiping away her tears, obviously distraught. She mouthed to Lindsay "I'm so sorry."

Lindsay flashed her a reassuring smile and mouthed back: "Don't worry." It wouldn't do anyone any good for Meg to be feeling guilty. She was doing her best. They all were.

When they got into the kitchen, Lindsay wrapped her mother in two fluffy blankets, and dried her hair with the blow-drier. She made them all a nice hot cup of steaming herbal tea, chatting cheerfully all the time about inconsequential matters.

Mrs. Richardson didn't seem any worse off for her little excursion. But the reality of how volatile the situation was at home struck Lindsay profoundly. And Meg seemed to be taking it really hard.

The sound of a car pulling into the driveway called her attention to the window.

"Aunt Charlotte!" Lindsay ran out to the driveway to meet her mother's sister. "What are you doing here?"

Although she was seven years younger than Mrs. Richardson, she actually looked much older. Lindsay always thought it was her white hair.

Wiping the snowflakes off her glasses with a ragged Kleenex, the registered nurse with a specialty in gerentology answered in her typically world-weary manner: "Meg called me. I came as soon as I could. What's going on?"

Lindsay led her into the house. "Mother took a little walk this morning."

"But she's okay? No falls, no chills..." She sat down in a kitchen chair next to Meg and Mrs. Richardson.

"So far, she's all right. And she's not at all frightened." Lindsay said.

"I should be doing more, Aunt Charlotte, but I don't know what to do or how to do it." They looked at Meg, whose voice was strong. "In the classroom, I know what the limits are, what the rules are, too. This scene changes every day, and we need to do what's best for Mom."

"You guys have to think about exactly that. Next time you might not be so lucky."

"I know you're right. We'll never forgive ourselves if something happens to her." Lindsay pulled out a chair and sat down with them.

"Do you really think you're able to take care of your mother?" The seriousness of Aunt Charlotte's message came through in her tone.

"We want to be," Meg tilted her chin up in the air.

"But there's only so much that two people can do. Your local Alzheimer Association might have some practical suggestions now."

"Like putting alarm chirps on the door jambs, so we'll know if they open," Lindsay said.

"But I think your physician is going to have to give you the big picture as far as today is concerned."

"We'll listen to you, Aunt Charlotte," Meg said firmly. "You're a professional, in nursing."

Lindsay nodded in agreement.

"I knew you'd feel terrible if we didn't call you," Meg added. "But sadly, it just feels like this is the beginning of the end."

"It feels like a new chapter in our life here has begun. And that's kind of scary." Lindsay said.

Aunt Charlotte moved toward the door. "Meg's right. It's a fork in the road, girls. So you guys know what your next moves are going to be. Good luck." She hugged them all. Mrs. Richardson beamed at her and held out her hands.

*Just let us do the right thing, Lord,* Lindsay prayed as she watched her aunt drive away. *I don't want any outsiders here. I'm afraid of what they'll do. What if they take her away? No one knows my mother better than Meg and me.*

Back in the house, her mother gave her a lovely tranquil smile. The image of that oil truck barreling around the corner, and the thought of the injuries that her mother could have sustained, haunted her thoughts.

If only her father could help them now. But then Lindsay was thankful that he had been so mercifully spared this anxiety. He never saw his wife sick. If he had, it might have broken his heart.

# *Chapter 5*

"You were supposed to be at that meeting with me. Where were you?" Dean's voice was low but Lindsay thought she saw a spark in his eyes.

Lindsay gripped the handle of her father's briefcase. Again. But this time, she was trying to keep her patience, not cowering before her new boss.

"I waited for you. Where were you?"

"I don't blame you for being mad. I'm sorry."

"Sorry?" Dean sounded like he couldn't believe his ears.

Lindsay moistened her lips, reliving her anxiety. "I was home."

"Home?"

"Yes," she said with a sigh. "I should have told you."

"Right." Dean was staring at her, as if another nose had popped out on her face right in front of him. "Somehow, Lindsay, you haven't struck me as the thoughtless type, but...hadn't you even wondered that I might be concerned or worried? How could you not think of that?" He removed his hands from his hips and waved them in the air as if he were conducting an orchestra. "What, then?"

"You can't imagine what I've been through." She walked over to the windows that overlooked the production facility.

"Tell me, please."

"Didn't Claire tell you?"

"No! So why don't you tell me, then?" he prompted. "We wouldn't want to start a trend of forgetting to tell me stuff."

Lindsay sat on the love seat. "Do you have any idea how the other half lives, Dean? Really?"

He moved towards her. "I'm not in the mood for a sermon, Lindsay. Can't you just talk to me?"

She sighed again and looked him right in the eye. He was right. "I had an emergency at home. My mother decided to go for a little walk all by herself. It's called wandering. Alzheimer's patients do it quite frequently."

A muscle twitched in Dean's neck. "Is she all right?" he asked.

Lindsay nodded, making sure to look more confident than she really felt.

"She's fine, we all are. The Richardsons are made of really good stock."

"No doubt there," he agreed.

"You really don't have to worry about us."

"I know."

"Or concern yourself with us."

"I know."

"So why'd you send us that basket of gladness? Not to sound ungrateful, Dean, but what made you do it?"

Dean seemed surprised. "You didn't like it?"

"Oh, it was a lovely gift. Thank you. The flowers, the treats...but I can't help but wonder why? It was kind of personal, if you think of it."

"Well, why not? You're a new employee and that's the kind of welcome we send to all our new hires."

"New hire?" Lindsay was amazed. Did he think she was a total rube? "So that's why you signed it the way you did?"

"Okay, you were friends with my father. It was friendlier than usual. Big deal."

She took a deep breath, remembering how much she needed this job. "I'm sorry I missed the meeting, Dean. Really. It won't happen again."

"Be sure it doesn't."

She moved to the door. "Okay. Thank you. And I apologize for causing you any unnecessary concern."

And as she walked out of his office, Lindsay hoped he wouldn't notice how unsteady she was on her feet. "I'll be in my office if you need me," she said.

"Lindsay," he called, his tone gentle. "I'm glad everything is okay."

"Thank you, Dean. I'm glad, too."

Lindsay glanced at the folder positioned on the passenger seat next to her. Since Meg, like most school teachers, kept neat and tidy records, Lindsay felt confident about giving the Treasurer's report for her at tonight's annual apartment owner's meeting.

Unlike earlier that day, she thought with a sigh. That episode had totally shaken her confidence. The events of her mother's adventure still sent chills up and down her spine. No wonder Meg had felt too sick to come to this meeting. Or did she, really? Lindsay suspected she was doing something else to help out the situation at home, like contacting the local Alzheimer's chapter, or having a handyman come over to help put chirpers on the doors.

She rang the bell at Dean's. He opened the door, and when he saw Lindsay a look of surprise lit his face.

"Lindsay! I wasn't expecting you--but come on in."

"Meg decided to stay home and take care of some things tonight, Dean, and she asked me to come in her place. Here's the Treasurer's report for the meeting."

"Are you just dropping this stuff off?"

"Oh no, I'll stay--if that's all right? I'd like to be able to tell Meg about the meeting, it being her apartment and all."

"Sure, Lindsay." He stepped aside as she moved into the marble-tiled entryway. She shrugged off her sheepskin jacket and jammed her matching gloves in her pocket.

"Something smell delicious!"

"I picked up some pizza for everybody. They'll be here soon."

Dean hung up her jacket and led her up the stairs to the living room where she saw two of the community's stony-faced residents propped on Dean's sofa.

"Mrs. Forsythe! And Nanette!" Lindsay smiled and held out her hand. "I'm Lindsay, Meg's sister. She couldn't make it tonight."

"We know who you are," Nanette said, checking her watch.

Mrs. Forsythe murmured, "Hello."

The doorbell rang and Dean ushered in three more residents, including the Vice President and the Recording Secretary of the apartment owner's association.

Ten minutes later the entire twenty-member community had assembled in Dean's contemporary living room. To Lindsay, it felt more like a wake than a meeting, the atmosphere so hushed and oppressive.

What a contrast the tense atmosphere was to the beautiful and warm furnishings in Dean's apartment. She admired original oils gracing the walls, and the gray and black furniture as well as three pieces of modern sculpture that could have just as easily been housed in the Rhode Island Art School Museum. But then she noticed, unlike his office, there was no copper in his home. There seemed to be one similarity, though: no personal photographs here, either.

The meeting called to order, Dean passed around copies of the agenda. Lindsay noted appreciatively only three items of business, so she should be able to get home soon.

The pizza sat steaming on the glass coffee table, the soda remained unsipped and the atmospheric pressure in the room seemed to be dropping by the second. Only the ticking of a brass and mahogany timepiece broke the stony silence as the residents reviewed the agenda.

Lindsay caught Dean's eye and angled her head.

"What's wrong?" she mouthed.

He shrugged his shoulders in response and she surmised he couldn't figure out why things felt so tense, either.

A few minutes later, Dean opened up the meeting, and before long, they were in the midst of their homeowner's issues.

"Well, we've covered the snow plowing issue, the roofing estimates and the decision not to proceed with a special assessment to build up our reserves. I'm proud of what we're doing here, even though this isn't my primary residence. Seems like we're right on top of things. " Dean kept his voice pleasant. "Before we hear the Treasurer's report, are there any miscellaneous items?"

The stony silence continued.

After what seemed to be an eternity, Mr. Collimore from Unit Three cleared his throat.

"On behalf of the group, Dean, yes. Yes, there are some issues we'd like to address."

"Need to address." Mrs. Forsythe's lips were tight.

Lindsay knew right away she hadn't misinterpreted the chill she had felt in the air.

"Of course," Dean said.

"Well, there seems to be some dissatisfaction--a great deal of dissatisfaction--among the residents here." Mr. Collimore looked up at Dean over the frame of his reading glasses.

"Concerning..."

"You. The problem seems to be you. On several layers."

Mrs. Forsythe gave a nervous cough.

"Really?"

There was genuine surprise in Dean's tone. The homeowners grumbled with dissatisfaction and mumbled among themselves.

Mrs. Chan from Unit One, bouncing her six-month old baby on her lap, spoke next.

"We're moving, Dean, because we want a yard for the baby. But there are things going on that we don't agree with and we think you should take care of."

"Well, let's hear it, friends. I'm your President. I want to know."

"But you don't represent us," snapped the biddy on the couch, Phyllis Cushman. "You just said it. You don't even live here. It's not your primary residence."

Mr. Collimore held up his hand. "Phyllis, please. Let's just proceed as we discussed."

Dean's eyebrows shot up in surprise. "Discussed? This is more like an ambush."

"It's really not a joke."

Lindsay couldn't tell who had said that, but there was no mistaking the disgust in their tone. Whatever happened to love thy neighbor?

She caught Dean's eye and tried to look supportive. From what she had seen of him in the past few days, she could easily imagine him rubbing folks the wrong way without even realizing he was doing so. He was a force to reckon with. Yet, deep down he wasn't a bad guy, at all. She knew it.

"The first issue, Dean, centers on your use of this unit as an unofficial party center for Copley Industries, offsite from your office. Instead of your primary residence." Mr. Collimore looked stern but Lindsay knew he was a mild-mannered gentleman at heart.

"After each and every Brown University football game, for instance, sixty or more partiers." Phyllis tisked. "Really."

At that point, everyone seemed to have a comment. "The traffic," said one resident. "The coming and goings," said another.

"And most of all, the noise," Phyllis threw her hands up in the air. "Our community is totally disrupted by you!"

"There are four games a year," Dean looked like he couldn't believe his ears. "And no one ever called me? I'm sorry you're disturbed. I'll change the venue, no problem."

"There's other issues," Mr. Collimore continued. "Dean, we question your leadership. Your accessibility. Your accountability. And most of all, your interest and commitment."

Lindsay felt the need to defend him, even though she wasn't really prepared to talk in front of everyone. "Tell me this, everyone." She stood up and heads turned to regard her in curiosity.

"Have any of you discussed these matters with Dean? Because there's nothing being mentioned we can't resolve here and now. I have the Treasurer's report from the owner's association right here to prove he's doing a good job." She waved her fistful of photocopies passionately.

"What do you know?" snapped Phyllis. "You don't live here."

"Sit down," someone else called.

Lindsay felt the color rise to her cheeks, but stood her ground.

"I will not sit down. Maybe I don't live here, but my sister Meg lives here and I represent her tonight."

An hour later, Dean closed the door behind the last resident and turned to Lindsay.

"Well aren't you the barracuda," he eyed her.

Shaking her head, she found her jacket in the closet and slipped it on. The meeting had taken longer than she had expected and she needed to get home.

"I hope I wasn't too forward, but I really needed to say what I did." She felt her cheeks redden.

Dean leaned against the doorframe. "Come on, Lindsay. You've got to let me thank you properly."

"There's no need to thank me, Dean, it's okay. I really have to get back to Meg and my mother. Are you all set with those dishes?"

"Maria will do them."

How foolish of her. Of course he had a housekeeper.

"How about coffee?"

"Maybe some other time."

"Maybe in Barringtown, now. That way you can check in at home and still make me happy."

"You're going to follow me all the way to Barringtown?"

Lindsay though she saw a twinkle in Dean's eye as he shrugged on his jacket. "I'm just too keyed up from all this excitement. And you have to tell me again how you got me to agree to host a holiday open house for everyone here in three weeks."

When they parked at Paris Express Cafe twenty minutes later, Lindsay pulled in next to Dean, who was waiting for her. Then they went in.

"There's not that much business here this time of night," Lindsay said confidently. "I know from living here that it's just a sleepy suburban bedroom community."

He held the door open for Lindsay, who looked at him wide-eyed when she saw the animated crowd.

"Come on." Dean pulled her through the group listening to the duet singing folk songs to a couple of chairs over by the gas-powered fireplace.

His cell phone went off while he was getting the attention of one of the wait staff that bustled over, disheveled and pink-cheeked from all the business.

"Hi there. I'll have an expresso. Lindsay?"

"A cappuccino, please." She pointed to his cell phone. "Does it ever stop ringing?"

"Not really." He shrugged. "Know what? There might be some way that Copley Industries can tap into all this late-night suburban restlessness."

"That sounds good, Dean. Do you mind if I just check in at home?"

He nodded. "Sure."

She dialed her home phone number.

"You know, speak to Claire about getting a laptop tomorrow."

"What do I need a laptop for?"

"Oh, believe me. You'll need it." He smiled a Cheshire cat smile.

Lindsay wondered what he meant by that, but kept her mind on the realities of home life. Lindsay couldn't understand why Meg hadn't picked up after three rings when finally Meg answered.

"Hi Meg. I'm here in Barringtown. At Paris Express. With Dean. I won't be long."

"Can you bring me an expresso?"

"Sure, call if you need me, I'll bring a hot cider for Mom. Love you." She rang off and gave Dean a big smile. "All set."

"Let me thank you for what you said." His eyes sparkled. "Ever since you walked in to my office you've been surprising me."

"Well, that's good. I guess, right?" She gave him a smile.

"I like surprises."

"Let me ask you something, Dean. Do you think you really see people for what they are? You might be a real target for people, Dean."

"Aren't all high-profile people, though?"

"People are jealous of your status. Your clout. Your wealth. I saw that tonight. You're a real target." She repeated, then smiled at the waitress serving them. "Thank you."

"No problem!" the java goddess replied, floating off into the crowd.

Just then Dean's cell phone went off. He checked the screen.

She sprinkled cinnamon over the whipped cream in her cappuccino. "I think it might be tough being you."

Dean pushed the disconnect button on his phone, then thoughtfully rubbed his lemon wedge around the rim of his cup.

"Most people would trade their world for the kind of world I live in faster than you could spell 'Copley'," he finally said.

She didn't miss the irony in his tone. And yet, who would believe it, with all the wealth he had? "You think so?"

"Not really. It's not everything you'd imagine."

"I have the picture," she said.

He shook his head. "Sorry I was so crappy to you this morning."

"Forget it. It's okay. I wasn't so great either. Maybe you just need something more fulfilling on a level that's going to mean something to you."

"I do tons of charity work."

"Yes, but not as Dean, it's always as Mr. Copley Industries."

"Hmmm. So what do you suggest?"

Lindsay thought for a moment. "It might be nice for you to get involved with something totally different from your work. Like Good Book Buddies..."

"I told you. I'll never try that. Me and kids...it's toxic."

"Cassidy didn't think so." She slanted him a look. "Or maybe even some of the activities in my church." Before he could scoff at the idea, she plowed on. "We're having a penny social next month. Maybe Copley Industries--or you--could think of some items to donate for us."

"Are you kidding?" Dean sounded unsure. "A penny social?"

"Don't worry. You won't need wire-rimmed glasses and an apron with marking pens. Just some time and thought on your part. To see if it makes you feel a little bit more enriched. On an abstract level."

"Not a material level."

"Exactly. Plus, we do need a Santa."

"Oh Lindsay, you'll never in a million years get me to dress up as Santa." Dean pointed his index finger at her, then wiggled it.

She smiled, then preteded to pout. "You're a natural actor, Dean. You never know."

In her heart of hearts, Lindsay felt convinced that this was just the sort of outlet he needed. True, he was busy. The cell calls this evening had shown her that. But Dean also seemed to be handling all his responsibilities very well. With time left over for coffee.

So no doubt, he had time left over for God. To give, to grow, to learn and to serve in the spirit. And maybe, just maybe, he would find that taking time to do these things would be taking time to learn how to love, too.

And what was that thought tugging at her heart about 'Do unto others'? Maybe she could reflect on what she was saying. Maybe she could use a little more of the Spirit in her to become more caring herself.

# *Chapter 6*

Lindsay looked at the ceramic platter and the cinnamon loaf she had positioned carefully on it.

*Not bad*, she thought, *but he's not the paper doily type.* He was too no-nonsense for that. She yanked the doily off the platter and tossed it, crumpled, into the trash.

"You'll never get me to play Santa!"

Remembrances of their talk the night before came back into her mind. There was just something too no-nonsense about him that told her he wasn't going to anything extra for anyone. Oh no, not Dean Singleton Copley. She could just imagine, with the kind of background he had.

Yet his father was very civic-minded, so he had a good example...she brought her thoughts back to the present and knocked on his copper doors, smoothing her suede skirt with her free hand.

"Come in, Lindsay," he called.

"How did you know it was me?"

"Claire calls, Gwynneth would never knock," he waved his hand in the air. "You're the only one."

Lindsay pondered this.

"Well, good morning anyway," she said brightly after a pause. "Meg baked this for you last night to apologize for not going to the meeting. Hope you like it." She turned to leave. "Have a good day."

"Wait a minute."

Dean rose from behind his desk to meet her midway before she walked out of his office.

"It means a lot to me, to think that someone would care enough to actually make something for me. Tell Meg I said thanks. You know, I ususally just order something over the phone. It smells delicious," he added with a smile.

She brightened. "Really? I'm not much of a chef, but Meg is. Give her anything to cook. She's fantastic."

"Here, let's try some." He appraised her dark green suit. "Nice outfit."

"Thank you." She wished he hadn't noticed, and wished it hadn't made her so glad to hear his approval. "It's not like life, though."

"What isn't?"

"Baking. I mean, don't you wish there was a recipe for life sometimes?"

Dean sliced the loaf thoughtfully. "There is a higher power."

Seeing his scarred hands reminded Lindsay of all he had been through.

"Do you believe that?" Holding the china dessert plate, she was unbelievably glad he seemed to be opening up to her.

Dean shrugged. "I have my moments."

She stifled a yawn. "Excuse me for that."

"Not my company, I hope?"

"Oh no! Sorry, Dean, I had a late night."

"Was your mother up again?"

On the one hand, she was sorry that he knew enough about her personal life to ask. But on the other hand, she was relieved that someone knew what she was going through. If only she could bury those feelings of wanting to get closer to Dean.

"No, thankfully. It's just that I seem to have a lot on my mind these days. Dean, do you ever feel pulled in more than one direction?"

"No. I'm always totally focused."

Lindsay felt that he had answered too quickly to really give the matter appropriate thought.

"Even though you're always so busy?" she probed.

"There's no doubt that there's a lot going on but--it's always work."

Maybe that was the problem. He was too much in control of what was going on in his world. And her world, on the other hand, seemed to be spinning totally out of control.

"Speaking of which," he continued "I have to go to London tonight and I'd like you to come with me. Is your passport current?"

She looked at him in amazement. "Passport? No. I don't have one."

"Well, you'd better get one if you're going to work here."

"All right. But isn't that requirement rather...specilaized?"

"No. I run a big business here."

"What about spontaneity, then, Dean?" She persisted, for reasons beyond her true understanding.

"In my world, there's no room for that. Can't you tell that everything is orchestrated?"

"And everything in my world is topsy-turvy now." She tried to lighten the mood. "Ironic, isn't it? Once again, we're opposites. These days, I just feel that my mother has to be my top priority."

Dean was looking at her when his phone buzzed.

"That's Claire. If you'll excuse me?" His tone was cool. "Why don't you get started on that day-care project with Gwynneth or something?"

"Sure."

Lindsay closed the door behind her.

As Dean watched her leave, he thought of his childhood, the endless string of nannies and housekeepers he had been under the charge of while his parents traveled through Europe, the long summers at overnight camp, the weekends at the summer homes of friends, the lack of homemade warmth and happiness. To put it in a nutshell, spontaneity had no place in his world. And neither had love. Until, maybe, now. Maybe something else was happening to change all of that now that Lindsay was around.

Mike was waiting for her after work in the bustling shopping arcade around the corner from Copley Industries Headquarters.

"Right on time," he said, in his flip tone Lindsay recognized as his personality trademark.

"I was anxious to get away from the office a little early for a while. Your call gave me the perfect excuse."

"Don't flatter me, Lindsay."

She laughed. "I'm only telling the truth."

They found a table under a trellis laced with flowering scarlet begonias.

Mike ordered a large pepperoni pizza and two sodas. "So how is it to work with the great Dean Singleton Copley, anyway? I only see him in passing."

She patted the laptop in the chic carrying case Claire had given her that morning. "He's very generous. Money is no object."

"But..."

She shrugged. "He's accommodating. And very hardworking. But I'm not sure his heart is really in it."

Mike scoffed. "There's a not-so-profound revelation!"

"What do you mean?"

"Why would he be really into it? He's only doing it 'cause of the accident."

Lindsay remembered the angry-looking scars on Dean's hands. "But that was twelve years ago, wasn't it?"

"Well, yeah, but I'm sure it feels like it just happened yesterday. You would, too, if it had been your fault." He saw her puzzled expression and continued: "You did know, didn't you, that he was the pilot that day?"

Lindsay took a deep breath, and then exhaled slowly. "No." Then Claire's words echoed in her mind: "Dean was piloting the chopper..." and she sighed. "I didn't put it all together..." *Maybe I've been too wrapped up in myself.*

"Well, he was. Oh yeah. Word is that Mr. Eager Beaver agitated to take the controls and Ronald said okay at the very last minute. But it turned out that the great Dean Singleton Copley was no top gun at all. And he's been trying to make up for it ever since." Mike took a slice of pizza and attacked it with gusto.

"Oh," Lindsay could just imagine the awful, wretched agony that Dean had put himself through since then. Her heart ached for him, and suddenly, so much of who he was and why he did things became clear to her. How could she have been so arrogant to him and showed so little compassion? She had been 'holier-than-thou' without meaning to. Ashamed of herself she looked at her lap. "Is he seeing someone?" she finally asked.

"That Gwynneth hangs around a lot."

"Professionally, Mike. Like a therapist."

"That I don't know. They've got me tracking him pretty closely, and I've never caught him coming out of any of that type of an appointment." He patted his camera. "But I'm always ready."

"Can you imagine what that's been like?" Lindsay was still reeling.

"I've got my own issues. Like paying my bills. This job calls me away all hours of the day and night. Makes a personal relationship very difficult." He put on a pathetic face. Suddenly he jumped up. "Speaking of which, here he comes."

Lindsay turned in her seat. Dean walked directly towards them. "Dean," she called, waving enthusiastically.

"Over here," Mike had his camera poised.

"Put that stupid thing down," she hissed, "and leave the guy alone."

Mike seemed to be surprised by her tone and did just what she said.

"Isn't this a nice spur-of-the-moment thing. Want to join me, Dean? Mike was just leaving."

Dean glanced at the half-eaten slice of pizza still on Mike's plate. "Why not? If I'm not interrupting. " He shot Mike a look. "Don't go blabbing to your editor. I don't want to read any surprises in tomorrow's paper from your chat. See you later."

"I'll call you Lindsay, we'll arrange that weekend trip."

Lindsay tisked, infuriated. "We will do no such thing," she called after him.

"So he annoys you, too," Dean observed.

"To no end." Her eyes twinkled. "But he's harmless."

She looked at him and jumped in, deciding to ignore the awkwardness of the moment. "What are you doing here?"

"I was picking up a few things on my way to the airport." He settled comfortably into a chair. "What are you doing here? With him? You should be on this trip with me."

"You know I can't hop off to London with things the way they are at home, even if I'd love to. You were right; he's been calling. He tried again this morning, and I said okay."

"Why?"

She held his gaze steadily. "I thought that getting out after work would clear my head a bit. I was very uncomfortable after I spoke with you this morning."

"Look," he raised his hands, "forget it. I'm sorry if I was too abrupt." He took a slice of pizza and bit into it. "I love pepperoni."

"Me too. And I'm sorry about this morning, too."

He smiled at her, that famous, heart-tugging, charismatic Copley smile that she hadn't let herself really see until then. It made Lindsay glad she was sitting down. She looked at the tabletop, hoping he would not tune in to how she was feeling about him. She could fall bad for this guy.

"Dean, you don't have to be sorry," she said after a pause. "But weren't you uncomfortable, too? I know you were."

"Not really."

"You acted like a different person."

Dean just shrugged.

"All right. But I felt bad because you were so different with me. I thought that perhaps I offended you when I asked you about spontaneity. It was only a question."

"I know. But I'm not one to talk about all that touchy-feeley stuff, Lindsay. I'm a businessman. A man of action. Don't you see?"

She nodded. "I guess so. But you're human, too, you know. Maybe it's a man thing."

When Dean didn't seem to have an answer to that, she continued. "You were great last night. You drove to Barringtown. I'd say that was pretty spontaneous."

"Just a little ride. I got swept up in the moment. The neighborliness, and then the coffeehouse made me feel like I was back in college."

She frowned. "You don't need to have a reason to feel things, Dean. You can just feel them. It is allowed, you know."

"There you go. Touchy-feeley. Ugh!" He raked his hands through his hair.

"I'll try to keep it light."

"Lindsay, you know my parents. You've seen my family in action. I think you can imagine what we're like. An uptight, status-conscious, embarrassingly wealthy bunch of freaks."

"You do have a way with words, Dean." Lindsay tried not to smile. "And you have a way with people, too. Despite yourself and the way you try to stifle it. I saw it with my mother when you came to the house, both times. You know, Alzheimer's patients have sort of a sixth sense about people. And they are very sensitive to their environments, and the atmosphere around them. Kind of like the way babies pick up on things, too. You know that Cassidy adores you. And my mother just melts."

Lindsay actually thought she saw the color spread across Dean's cheeks. But maybe it was just the lighting in the arcade. She couldn't be sure.

"This was pretty spontaneous," she said.

He nodded his agreement. "There's something I really want to tell you. I was thinking about that penny social you mentioned last night. Two things." He looked at her.

"What?" She finished her pizza and took a sip of soda, willing her quickening heartbeat to cool down.

"First, Copley Industries has a lot of stuff we could donate. I'll have Claire draw up a list and give it to you. You can check off what you want and then we'll make an appointment to go over it. And you will never, ever, get me to play Santa."

"Okay, or, we could just talk about it when you get back."

He nodded. "I know what you're getting at, Lindsay. You think I'm too structured. And maybe you're right. We'll get to that."

"Sounds good," she smiled. At least it was a start. "I don't mean to be too pushy, Dean, really. I am so bossy and I'm sorry. It's a major fault of mine and I'm trying to work on it."

"Good." He eyed her. "The second thing is the larger picture you were referring to. I think you're right and I'd like to maybe get involved in something a little more meaningful than work. Maybe."

"Maybe is a good place to start, that's what I always say. In my bossy way." Lindsay's heart soared at the prospect of Dean finding a bit more fulfillment in his life through forming an association with her church.

Dean's cell phone went off just then.

He answered it and the color drained from his face.

"Rhode Island Hospital? I'll be right there!" he cried, panic in his voice. Passersby and patrons turned to look at him.

Lindsay grabbed his arm. "Dean! What's wrong?"

He looked at her, wild with concern, raw fear filling his eyes. "It's my father. He's had a heart attack and they're not sure he's going to make it. I've got to go!"

"I'm coming with you," she cried after him, tossing some bills on the table to cover the cost of their meal. "Wait, Dean! I'll drive you!"

# *Chapter 7*

Lindsay drove as if her life depended on getting to the hospital. Luckily, she was able to find a parking space right away.

They rushed into the lobby and found out Dean's father was in Emergency surgery, and if he survived he would be transferred to the ICU.

*Dear Lord, please watch over them all*, she prayed to herself. The Copleys needed every prayer they could get at this point.

The smell of antiseptic in the hallway and the glare of fluorescent lights were all too familiar to Lindsay and brought all the pain of her father's death back to her. She hoped that Dean didn't have to experience what she'd gone through. But if he did, she'd be there to help him as much as she could.

"All we can do now is wait." She put her coat down on an empty chair in the waiting area outside the ER, noticing two other clumps of people, one couple clinging together and sobbing uncontrollably. A glance at Dean's pale face told her how upset he was.

"Where is everyone?"

"I'm sure they're on the way. They'll be here soon." Lindsay tried to stay calm.

Dean walked down the linoleum hallway away from her, cell phone clutched to his ear. He stopped at a vending machine then came back and joined her, handing her a can of soda. "Here, Lindsay." He sat next to her and ran his hands through his hair. "I called Claire. She said my mother and Kathy were on the way."

"Will she be coming, too?"

"Probably." His sigh was deep and weary. "Now it's time for the 'if-only's'."

She frowned, unsure of his meaning.

"If only I had said this, or done that, or tried more..." he explained.

"Don't do that to yourself, Dean. You're a good son."

He shook his head.

"Not really. I'm just trying to make it look that way." He stared at her intently. "Like I have for the past twelve years."

"Since the accident."

He nodded. "You heard about it."

"Claire filled me in a bit. And Mike did, too. I'm so sorry, Dean." She spoke softly. "I can only imagine the pain you've been in. But I know your father is very proud of you. Your whole family is. And they should be proud of you." She spoke with conviction.

He looked at her in disbelief.

"How can you say that? I'm a total failure, Lindsay! I killed my own brother and I'll never forgive myself. And they'll never forgive me, either. Deep down."

"No, Dean, that's not true."

"It is true." His voice seethed in quiet pain. "All of it is."

He looked at the floor. "You don't understand. Ronald was the shining star of this family. We're Copleys. Very competitive. We all excel in different areas, but put us together and Ronald was still head and shoulders above us all. All-state athlete in three sports, two graduate degrees, a volunteer at the soup kitchen he founded..." His voice cracked. "...an accomplished pilot..."

"Oh, Dean, I'm so sorry..."

"I know they resent me for it. How could they not? They're trying to accept me, but they don't feel the same as they did before the accident. Especially my father."

As he raised the soda to take a drink, Lindsay noticed the ugly scars once again. He continued, his voice subdued. "I don't know why I insisted on flying that day. I knew Ronald was better. But I never thought that I'd cause anything like I did."

He paused, and said, almost as if he were thinking out loud: "I don't deserve their forgiveness. I have everything a man could ever want, all the material things you could ever imagine. And I don't deserve any of it. I don't deserve to be in this family, a family I've all but destroyed. Not only that, I'm not worthy of their forgiveness, either. Or their love."

Lindsay blinked back the tears that were stinging her eyes. "'Love bears all things', Dean, 'believes all things, hopes all things, endures all things'." She let the words from Corinthians speak to Dean in the way that he needed to hear.

He looked at her, pain furrowing his brow. "I'm just trying to make it up to them. They deserve it. It's my responsibility."

She nodded. "But you also have a responsibility to yourself, Dean. A right to be happy."

"I have no right to that at all."

"Yes, you do. God wants it for you. He wants you to be happy."

He took a deep breath. "I've always believed that, Lindsay. But it's been kind of hard lately."

She nodded and was just about to mention how faith can touch our lives when a middle-aged physician in operating room scrubs approached the waiting area.

"I'm looking for the family of Mr. Copley?"

"Yes?" In one synchronized move, Dean and Lindsay jumped out of their seats.

"I'm Dr. Greene. Your father is one tough, strong man. We almost lost him but he's not ready to go. We had to put in a stent, and now we're moving him to recovery." His smile was broad. "You'll be able to see him soon."

"When can he come home?"

"We'll watch him for a day or two, and if all goes well, we'll see. But he'll be home by Christmas."

"Thank you so much, Dr. Greene," Dean shook his hand vigorously.

"Good luck to you and your family," he said with a smile and then hustled down the hall.

"Oh, Dean," Lindsay was overjoyed. "I'm so glad. Thank God."

A while later, Dean came back from the nurse's station and found Lindsay and Claire in the waiting room outside of recovery.

"He's going to room 725. It's private, which will be nice."

"How's he feeling?" Claire put down her knitting to look at Dean.

"Well, he's groggy, as you'd expect. But he's glad he made it." He looked down the hall. "Did Mom and Kathy get here?"

"Not yet." Claire's tone was frosty. "I did call and leave them messages. Twice."

"If they get here, they can come in and see him. But it's only immediate family now. I'd apologize, but the irony is too funny to even take seriously."

Claire continued, lips tight and her tone businesslike.

"I asked them to bring some of Mr. Copley's things, you know, to make him more comfortable. Maybe that's what is taking them so long. Would you like me to go out and get him some personal items, Dean?"

"That would be great, Claire."

"I'll get going, too," Lindsay stood as well.

"No, you stay here." Dean insisted. "He was asking for you especially," he murmured out of earshot of Claire.

Lindsay blushed, touched by the thought of Mr. Copley's remembrance of her. "I want to see him, too. I'm glad you had a chance to see him privately."

"Me, too. Thank you, Claire." He hugged her quickly before Claire bustled off down the hall.

Room 725 was ready sooner than they had expected. Dean came by and told Lindsay, "He wants to see you now." He flashed her his very first smile during the ordeal.

She walked to his bed, a million thoughts racing through her mind. "Mr. Copley." She held out her hands to him and he took them, smiling at her.

"Darling?"

The door to the room swung open and Mrs. Copley and Kathy stood there, dramatically framed in their floor-length fur coats.

"What have they done to you? We were at Steven's. We came as soon as we could."

"Steven's, the hairdresser?" Lindsay couldn't believe it.

"Daddy!" Kathy cried, rushing over to Mr. Copley's bedside, nearly pushing Lindsay out of the way. But Mr. Copley kept a firm hold on her hand, keeping her in place.

"It's time for family, now." Mrs. Copley's tone was haughty. "Thank you, and all the employees of Copley Industries, for your care and concern."

Lindsay thought Mrs. Copley sounded like she was making an acceptance speech at the Academy Awards. She didn't miss the dismissal in her look.

Taking special care to keep her tone pleasant, Lindsay said: "I was just leaving. Be sure to do what the doctors tell you, Mr. Copley. I'll check in with you later."

"Thank you, my dear." He kissed her hand appreciatively. "Thank you for being here with me. And for being with Dean."

She left the room to join Dean in the hall and found herself confronted with another shock--Gwynneth wrapped around Dean like a boa constrictor!

She noticed how his arms were hanging limp, by his side, and nearly laughed at the 'please save me' look he flashed at her.

Before she could warn Dean what was coming, Mike suddenly appeared from around the corner and snapped four quick shots before scuttling away.

"Why, that creep," Dean sounded furious.

But he did not see the look of smug satisfaction on Gwynneth's face. Lindsay, however, didn't miss it. She knew that Gwynneth had set him up!

"I'm going now, Dean," she called casually, "can I drop you off somewhere?"

"That would be great. Let me say bye to Dad." Extricating himself from Gwynneth's hold, he dashed away like a jackrabbit.

Gwynneth kept her back to Lindsay, yet Lindsay heard her say: "You'll never get him. He's mine and everyone knows that."

What, did he come with papers, like a show dog? Lindsay found her patience, and composed herself before replying.

"Don't fret, Gwynneth. You know I'm not in your league. And Dean knows, too." She knew Gwynneth was too self-centered to understand the irony of what she really meant.

Besides, she thought, as they headed towards the parking lot, she didn't want to "get" Dean. She looked at his profile from the corner of her eye. Walking next to her as they went to her car, he was unusually quiet, and deep in thought.

No, she didn't want to "get" him. And yet, for some reason, it bothered her more than she wanted to admit to consider the prospect of not having Dean in her life.

But she didn't have time to analyze that just now. She'd just have to let God help her figure it out.

What was that feeling tugging at her heart?

"There's not much to work with here."

Lindsay cast a forlorn look into Dean's refrigerator. Milk, a few cans of soda, half a loaf of bread, some romaine, an apple and a half-empty carton of orange juice. "How about the pantry?"

"Pantry?"

Lindsay laughed. "Okay, I guess modern penthouses like these don't have 'pantries'...But where do you keep your supplies?"

Dean shrugged, sheepishly. "I eat out a lot, and I take home a lot of prepared foods."

"We'll manage." Lindsay found ziti and a jar of marinara sauce. She made garlic toast, a salad with apple and walnuts, and a big bowl of steaming pasta.

"And you did dessert, too?" Dean asked, coming in to sit down. "This set-up is something I could get very used to."

"You had a box of pudding, so I used it with the last of the milk."

"Wow." Dean was obviously impressed. "I was just on the phone with Dad. He had turkey for dinner. When he comes home, maybe I can ask him over here."

Lindsay beamed. "What a great idea! You guys should get together more."

Dean cleared his throat. "I meant with you here, too."

They wanted her there with them? Lindsay was too surprised to answer. But her thumping heart told her plenty.

After a pause, she managed: "Oh. Sure!"

There was another pause before Dean spoke.

"Maybe you can stop by and visit him tomorrow. He likes you."

"By all means."

Lindsay stacked the dirty dishes in the sink. "Wash or dry?"

"Both. You've done enough." Dean's tone was firm.

She frowned at him, but he just smiled.

"You know, Lindsay. You have a way with people. I can see how soothing it must be for your mother whenever you're around. You have a good effect on people."

"Why, thanks...You do too, Dean."

"It seems to suit you, too. I mean you seem to like it."

She nodded her agreement. "True. I do love it."

"It seems like you were born to do it. You're so natural at it." As he helped her get her coat on, Lindsay wanted to hug him more than anything. But something held her back.

"See you tomorrow, Lindsay. Drive safely. And thanks for everything."

She wondered if she should hug him, but decided that her emotions had to be kept in check. She didn't want him to misinterpret any of her actions, or her words.

"Let me know if you guys need anything," she said brightly, keeping her tone light and her expression upbeat.

As she drove through the night, she couldn't help but wonder what the future held for all of them. And what would be waiting for her at home.

# Chapter 8

"Let's read this one, Lindsay!"

Seven-year-old Matthew Graham, wearing a bright plaid shirt and brand-new khakis, held up a volume in the "Thinking Like Jesus" series. The filtered noontime sunlight warmed the room, highlighting the streaks in Matthew's brown hair.

"Good idea." She held the book for him as he took a sip of his chocolate milk and began reading the updated story of the Good Samaritan.

She caught Claire's eye across the classroom and they gave each other a satisfied smile. Lindsay noted with interest that Claire seemed very well matched with her child, and eight-year-old girl from nearby Bristol named Edila.

"Keep reading, Matthew," Lindsay urged as he munched politely on his fish sticks. The boy complied easily, sounding out the words that were unfamiliar to him.

"...As they traveled along the road..." Lindsay listened attentively to her Bible Good Book Buddy, thinking about how far each of the eight children in the program had come since their beginning in September.

Suddenly, the classroom door opened, generating a flurry of curiosity throughout the peaceful classroom.

She looked to the door and her heart gave a lurch. It was Dean. What in the world was he doing here?

❧ ❧ ❧

"Can I help you?"

Mrs. Cordeiro, the Good Book Buddy coordinator, waddled over to him, glancing protectively over her shoulder at her eight small charges.

"I'm Dean, a new volunteer, and I've been matched up with..." he referred to the paper in his hand. "With Kodi. I'm Kodi's new Good Book Buddy."

"Nobody told me Kodi was joining the program."

She eyed Dean suspiciously and plucked the paper from his fist. "Otherwise I'd have him here all ready for you. He must be down in the cafeteria. I'll go get him."

"Thank you so much, ma'am," Dean's tone was honey-sweet.

And it worked. Mrs. Cordeiro's smile lingered on him.

Dean watched her bustle off down the corridor. Then he looked over at Lindsay, who seemed to be totally focused on her buddy Claire, too seemed engrossed.

Then he caught Lindsay's eye. She beamed at him. Claire, too, looked up and smiled.

"There's another bigger chair in the room next door, for when the poppa bears visit," a little voice chimed.

A chorus of giggles followed.

"And here's Kodi!" Mrs. Cordeiro announced triumphantly as she produced a little blonde guy in jeans and a turtleneck sweater. "He's all done eating, so you two can just get acquainted. Kodi, here's your new Book Buddy, Dean."

"Hey, dude." Dean produced three books and settled Kodi into a chair next to him. "We're different sizes but we both love books in a big way." Dean felt a tightening around his heart that had never happened before. He looked into Kodi's big blue eyes and the youngster gave him a lopsided smile. Wow.

Lindsay heard them talking and tried to keep her attention focused on Matthew.

A few minutes later, however, she looked Dean's way and caught his eye. He gave her a smile. It was so filled with hope that it tugged at her heart.

She nodded and smiled back at him, not caring if he saw how thrilled she was inside.

All too quickly, the Good Book Buddy hour had come to an end. As the children returned their trays to the cafeteria, Dean caught up with Lindsay and Claire.

"Are you ladies glad to see me?"

"Very, Dean. I'm glad you're here."

"I had a feeling you'd come. I was hoping." Claire added.

"Did you walk here, Dean?" Lindsay wondered.

"I had the taxi drop me off after my other meeting across town."

"Want to come back with us?"

"You're ever-practical Lindsay," Dean's voice sounded warm.

"Aren't we all lucky she's around," Claire said with a smile.

Dean made a call on his cell phone, then hopped into the back seat of Lindsay's Toyota.

"Tell us what you thought, Dean. What are your impressions?" Claire probed.

"It was nice," Dean said enthusiastically. "Kodi's a great kid."

"What story did you read?"

"The story of Cain and Able. It was one that Kodi really seemed to enjoy."

Lindsay didn't say anything, but wondered if Dean had chosen that story on purpose. Were there similarities to his own life?

"We read the Woman at the Well," Claire offered.

Lindsay gunned the Camry through a crowded intersection, turning right at the red light. "We read the Good Samaritan again."

"Matthew loves that one." Claire filled Dean in.

"That's one story you really can't read too many times." Dean said.

Lindsay shot him a glance from the corner of her eye to see if he was making fun of them. He didn't seem to be and she flashed him a smile as she parked the car back at the office.

"Back to the salt mines," he said with a chuckle. "See you later, ladies." He dashed off toward the building while Lindsay and Clair gathered their things and headed back inside after him.

When she got back to her desk she checked her voice mail while munching on an energy bar snack.

"Three new messages." the automated voice reported.

She rolled her eyes at the first one, Mike, and erased it promptly. The second one, from Mrs. Copley, generated more interest on her part.

"Lindsay we're so appreciative of all your help at the hospital during Mr. Copley's emergency. Won't you please join us for lunch Saturday at the Ivy Club and let us show you, in some small way, how much your kindness has meant to us all."

Lindsay wondered why she would extend herself after being so cool to her every time they had met in person.

She dialed the number Mrs. Copley had left, curious to follow through on the invitation. A woman who identified herself as Mrs. Copley's secretary answered, and when Lindsay explained the reason for her call, she replied: "Wonderful, Ms. Richardson. Mrs. Copley will be so delighted."

"Well, that's nice," Lindsay replied, "I'll be looking forward to meeting her then."

The third message was from the secretary at her church. "Call us, Lindsay," she said. "We're concerned about your recent activities and the publicity you've been stirring up."

*Oh, boy*, she thought. *Just what I need, a confrontation with my parish*. She was glad it was a recorded message. She'd have to call them back later.

She said a silent prayer for guidance while she drove home. When Lindsay arrived, Meg met her at the door with a worried look on her face.

"Mom's not eating, Lindsay. I hate to tell you this, but things aren't so great here. Aunt Charlotte's on her way over now."

❧ ❧ ❧

"Well, I'm really glad you girls called me. I had no idea your mother was this bad."

Aunt Charlotte removed her glasses, breathed her own steam on the lenses, then wiped them with an old tissue. She and Lindsay were standing outside her car in the driveway.

Lindsay sighed. "With all your experience as Head of the Visiting Nurse's Association, Meg and I knew you were the one to call. I just wish it was for something happy, though, like it used to be." She glanced at the kitchen window, to see if her mother was moving around. Remembering the old family times together, it was so hard to think they would never happen again.

"We're here, Sam." Aunt Charlotte's voice was soothing, and the poodle in the back seat closed his eyes and curled up into a ball of contentment.

"He's so cute." As she said it, Lindsay knew how lame it sounded.

"She's really a lot further along than I imagined." Her aunt eyed her cautiously. "It's just that sometimes these patients develop other illnesses, too. That's something you have to watch out for. As well-meaning as you girls are, you're not professionals."

Lindsay shook her head, shivering from nerves as much as the cold. "I'm so worried about her, Aunt Charlotte."

"I know."

"The Visiting Nurses will help, I'm sure. Doctor DiNunzio called me this morning and told me they'd be starting on our case tomorrow around three. They'll help us be as proactive as we can be."

Sam's yipping resumed, annoying Lindsay to no end. "You're getting cold, Aunt Charlotte," she prompted.

"What about Meg?"

"She's worried sick but putting on a brave front. You know how strong she is. How can it not take its toll on her, though, too?"

"How sad." Aunt Charlotte placed a hand lovingly on Lindsay's arm. "If you need help with anyone or anything." She gave Lindsay a meaningful look. "Call me."

"We will. Thank you, Aunt Charlotte." The two kissed warmly, and Lindsay dashed into the house.

The warm, cozy kitchen welcomed her cheerfully. She hugged her mother, wondering how much longer she and Meg would be able to keep her living at home. What was God's plan for them? What she wouldn't give to be able to ask her mother what to do right now. It was painfully ironic to Lindsay that her mother was there, in her arms...but because of the Alzheimer's, she was not really there, at all.

"What's wrong, Lindsay?"

Claire put the morning mail on Lindsay's desk and took a seat across from her. Bright, dazzling sunlight filled the room, masking the November chill outside.

"I'm just so distracted, Claire. My mother seems to be getting worse. I'm so anxious." She drummed her fingers nervously on her desk.

"That's understandable."

"I don't know what to do. The Visiting Nurse is coming today at three."

"So you have to leave early."

Lindsay nodded.

"I think you'll feel better after you speak with her, Lindsay. At least you and your sister will have some sort of assessment. It will help you determine what the future has in store."

"It's so hard not knowing."

But what she didn't mention to Claire was part of the 'not knowing' she was talking about was not knowing if her job at Copley Industries had precipitated this recent decline in her mother. She couldn't help but feel if she had been with her mother all day, every day, as she had been in the recent past, perhaps her mother would have been doing better. Oh, she had read all about Alzheimer's and how it progresses, regardless of what loved ones did. But she couldn't help but wonder, deep in her heart, about it.

"I have to go tell Dean." She stood, smoothing the front of her black skirt.

"Good luck," Claire said.

*Lord, let me find the words for what I need to say*, she prayed as she tapped on Dean's door.

"You don't need to knock, Lindsay," he called.

Walking into his office reminded her of that first day, not so long ago. She had opened the wrong door, or at least her self-doubts had led her to believe so, back then. But maybe in a weird way it had been the right door for her. So many things had changed since, and she had learned so much about Dean.

Her heart pounded as she saw him take his stance, concentrating before he sank his putt.

"All right," he whooped, "four in a row!"

"Pretty good."

He turned to Lindsay. "I bet you couldn't do it."

The last thing in the world she wanted to do was have a putting contest with Dean. "You're absolutely right."

"Aren't you the all-business type this morning. You've got to lighten up, Lindsay, like you've told me. See, I've listened to you. Ease into things here. It makes for a more productive day. Business Management 101."

"Duly noted for the record, Dean. Now can I talk to you?"

He raised one eyebrow. "Sure you can. Are you quitting?"

She shook her head. "I hope not. I don't want to. But I'm concerned about things at home. My mother seems to be developing some problems, and the Visiting Nurse is coming today at three to see her." She coughed a dry and nervous cough.

"Like what's happening?"

"Her appetite is dwindling, which is major. She won't take her pills. She seems to be getting weaker..." Lindsay sighed.

"Sounds iffy, Lindsay."

She nodded. Why was her mouth so dry? "I need to be there."

"No problem. Want a ride home? I'll have Howard take you if you want." Lindsay knew that Howard, Dean's driver, was always ready to take someone anywhere they needed to go.

She dismissed the thought with a wave of her hand. What was that funny stinging in her eyes?

"Are you okay, Lindsay?" Dean's voice sounded like it was coming from very far away. She tried to swallow, but couldn't.

The next thing she knew she was in a heap in Dean's arms, crying her eyes out.

"Are you going to pass out? Come here." Gently, Dean guided her over to the love seat. "Boy, Lindsay, you are light as a feather. Come on now, it'll be okay."

Producing his handkerchief, he mumbled, "Between spills and now tears, I can't believe how many of these I've gone through since you started here."

She said something that only came out in an agonized wail.

Patting her knee, he said, "There, there, Lindsay. I'm sure it will be okay."

"I wish it wasn't necessary," she sniffed through her tears. "I wish things were the way they used to be."

Taking her in his arms he murmured, "I know, I know. I know just how you feel. I've felt like that for years. Longing for the past, for what could never be recaptured. But you know, Lindsay, when things get worse for your mother, what will you girls do? You can't wait for the crisis to start. It's good that you're being proactive."

"You just can't imagine how awful I feel," she sobbed into his shoulder.

"It's okay to be sad..."

"Maybe it's my fault. Because I haven't been with her."

He cupped her tearstained face in her hands and gazed into her eyes. "Don't do this to yourself, Lindsay. Remember what you told me? That I'm a good son? Well, you're a good daughter. And you know Alzheimer's just progresses, regardless of what anyone does or doesn't do."

Lindsay liked his tone of voice. She focused on him and hiccoughed softly. "That's not just lip service?" She blinked away more tears.

"It's from my heart."

As he watched her walk down the corridor, Dean pondered this recent development. What he had said to Lindsay was straight from his heart. Little did she know how true his words were.

For in talking to her now, and hopefully comforting her just a little, Dean realized just how much she had helped him in the past few days. And he realized how much she had come to mean to him.

Could this be what they meant by love?

Lindsay opened the door at three o'clock to find a short, plump nurse with a round face and an endearing smile standing there, waiting for her. Lindsay thought she looked like an angel.

"I'm Melissa Hamilton." She took Lindsay's hand in both of hers. "No doubt in my mind that you're Mrs. Richardson's youngest, Lindsay."

"I'm sure my mother will love you."

"Good. We want her to be happy." She lowered her voice and patted Lindsay's hands reassuringly. "And don't you worry. We know how to handle families in crisis. We run into it all the time. People get overwrought because they care so much about their loved ones."

She breezed into the kitchen where Meg and Mrs. Richardson were waiting.

Shaking Meg's hand, she said "I'm Melissa, your mother's nurse." Then she turned all her attention to Mrs. Richardson. "How are you today?"

Mrs. Richardson smiled, and Lindsay said a little prayer of thanksgiving to the Lord.

"She seems wonderful," she whispered to Meg, seated next to her.

"Mom seems to like her, which is all I care about." Meg dabbed at her eyes with a raggedy Kleenex.

Melissa finished her examination of Mrs. Richardson, then sat at the kitchen table with the three of them.

"You're both Mrs. Richardson's full-time caregivers?"

Meg and Lindsay nodded.

"All right, then." She closed her notebook with authority and recapped her pen with a brisk and efficient 'snap'.

"Here's what we're going to do. I've made my report for the doctor. You keep a file copy, and then he reviews my recommendation. If he agrees, my VNA superiors then get the final review, and the wheels start turning. You gals are doing a wonderful job here. What I'm recommending is one visit per week for the next four weeks, then a reassessment of Mrs. Richardson's state at that time."

"So you'll be back next week?" Meg asked.

"Yup. And now, if anything develops, at least we have a baseline set of stats. Three heads are better than two, so to speak."

They shared a smile, and Lindsay said a prayer of thanks to God. The atmosphere in the kitchen seemed a lot lighter.

"Let's go!" Mrs. Richardson called.

Melissa gave a genuine laugh.

"You're exactly right, Mrs. Richardson. I've outstayed my welcome here."

"All right!" Mrs. Richardson called, to no one in particular.

"I can see why the doctor said you were a close family," Melissa looked from one to the other. "To see this kind of closeness in a family is truly heartwarming."

Lindsay got up and said good-bye, then Meg followed suit. Melissa gave them each one of her business cards, and told them not to hesitate to call if they needed anything.

After she had pulled out of the driveway, Lindsay grabbed Meg and hugged her. Meg hugged her back, extra tight, which made her feel good.

"I feel like dancing!" Lindsay exclaimed. "Can you believe how nice she is? We have hope now, Meg. Oh, say your prayers of thanksgiving to God for sending her to us."

"I will, Lindsay. But it's hard to feel grateful when the reason we're going through this is because Mom's is so sick. I can't understand why God is doing this to her. And don't get too palsey-walsey with this nurse, yet. You don't really know her."

"I know you're right. But my heart is still overjoyed." Lindsay desperately wanted to share her faith with Meg, but kept coming up against a solid wall of disbelief and resistance. "Don't you think this is good for Mom, though, Meg?"

Meg sounded thoughtful when she eventually spoke. "I think we're doing the right thing. But I think God is really wrong for making her sick. That's why my heart keeps breaking into more and more sad little pieces, and why I am barely able to do anything. I've loved God my whole life, Lindsay. You know that. And I've never been angry with Him. Not even when He took Daddy." She sighed. "But I'll never forgive God for this."

# *Chapter 9*

"You never had a chance to tell me what made you show up at Book Buddies, Dean." Lindsay crunched through the golden carpet of leaves lining the walkway to the Ivy Club. Saturday had dawned crisp and clear, a beautiful late autumn day.

Dean tried to sound casual. "I just thought I'd give it a try. It seems to make you and Claire so happy."

Lindsay angled her head as they reached the Club, a sprawling, impressive brick mansion strategically located on a corner lot atop College Hill, affording one of the most sweeping views of the city of Providence. She wasn't sure he was telling her the whole truth. Her instincts told her his reasons were deeper...but she couldn't pull it from him. He had to tell her on his own.

"Here we are," he said, opening the door for her. With its ivy-covered exterior and beautifully landscaped grounds, the building exuded an imposing aura of privilege, status, and old New England money that carried through into the design of its classic, antique-laden interior.

"It's very nice," she said. But inside, she was feeling a little intimidated. She hadn't ever been in a private club such as this before.

"It's kind of stodgy, but I won't sway you." His eyes twinkled mischievously. "I know you have a mind of your own."

"How right you are," she answered. "I have to try and be open-minded, not headstrong. Plus, my confidence falters sometimes, you know."

Dean smiled and guided her across the richly carpeted floors into one of the mansion's front parlors. A cozy fire crackled in the fireplace, seasonal ornamentation decorating the massive marble mantle. Rows of leather-bound first editions glowed in beautiful mahogany floor-to-ceiling bookcases, which gleamed as the afternoon sun filtered through oversized windows nearby.

"We're here," Dean announced.

Simultaneously, Mrs. Copley and Kathy turned in their wing-backed chairs to face them.

Kathy hopped up and greeted them warmly.

"Welcome to the Club. Looking pretty dapper, there, Dean," she teased. "How are you, Lindsay?"

"Fine, thanks," Lindsay answered, although she felt anything but fine. It was too hot. She was totally out of place. Why wasn't there anyone else in the parlor? Eyeing Kathy's smartly tailored pants suit, she knew she was dressed all wrong. She should have been on Hee Haw, not at the Ivy Club.

She shook Kathy's smooth, dainty hand, managing: "How are you?"

"Wonderful," Kathy carelessly tossed her raven black waves back over a thin shoulder.

"And when are you not?" Dean's eyebrow elevated.

"Pish, tosh, Mr. Dry Humor!" Kathy said with a smile that Lindsay thought looked like an advertisement for cosmetic dentistry.

"I brought these for you." Lindsay thrust two little gift bags forward, feeling that their humble contents were insufficient for such grand folks as the Copleys.

"Oh look, Mummy, Lindsay brought us gifts." Kathy moved to show her mother.

Lindsay noticed that Mrs. Copley had remained in her chair, planted. She looked at Dean, wondering if she should go over to her. That stained-glass seminar at the crafts store she was missing for this luncheon was sounding real good to her about now.

Dean moved over to his mother. "How are you, Mom?"

"Very well, Dean, thank you. Hello, Lindsay."

"How nice to see you, Mrs. Copley."

"Mmmm! Lavender sachet. Thank you, Lindsay." Kathy smiled sweetly."That reminds me, Mummy. Are we going to Opulent Treasures after lunch?"

"You know I have an appointment at Steven's at three."

"But I thought we had this all set," Kathy whined.

"We had nothing of the sort. Alvaro's didn't take us until eleven."

"But last week you said I could buy..."

"Ladies?" Dean's tone of voice got their attention instantly.

"Oh, sorry." Kathy said.

"Sit down right here, both of you," Mrs. Copley ordered, indicating a love seat upholstered in striped satin. Her voice boomed through the quiet of the refined Club, and left no room for discussion.

"Right next to me," Dean prompted, patting the cushion next to him.

A member of the discreet wait staff approached them.

"What would you like for a beverage, Lindsay?" Mrs. Copley asked.

"Club soda's fine, thank you." Trying to stay poised even though she felt a little nervous, she shifted her focus to the server.

"Me, too," Dean chimed in. He flashed Lindsay a knowing smile.

"I'm glad your mother is well enough for you join us, today. Dean has told us all about your situation. How uncertain it is from day to day."

"It sounds really tough," Kathy offered solicitously.

From the sound of her voice, Lindsay could tell that she could hardly imagine what was going on, but, at the same time, was trying to show that she cared about it. No matter what she really thought, Lindsay found that someone who cared was endearing.

"The circumstances are unusual, there's no doubt about that. But we're a close family, and between me and my sister, we pretty well manage to take care of things."

Mrs. Copley took a long draw on her drink, not losing eye contact with Lindsay for an instant.

"I've been taking care of my mother for years, Lindsay, and it has not been easy."

Lindsay nodded. "I can imagine."

"And I'll tell you something else. If I couldn't afford to have live-in help around the clock when your father got out of the hospital, I'd have to place him in a home. I won't sugarcoat it, Dean. That's the reality of it. Yes, I've succeeded in keeping my marriage intact and raising children. But my life has never really been my own."

"But surely you must feel some relief in the fact you've done what's right, Mrs. Copley, don't you?" Lindsay really wanted to know.

"No, I don't. I do not believe it is a child's place to take care of a parent. Such is not why they are put on God's green earth. And it's not the life I've planned for either of my children."

Lindsay looked down at her drink, embarrassed beyond words. She knew Mrs. Copley was warning her off her son. "Parents want the best for their children, Mrs. Copley. But children grow up and make their own decisions."

"Some children don't have the chance to grow up." Mrs. Copley answered.

Remebering the tragedy the family had been through, and that this woman had lost her son, Lindsay felt absolutely awful. Let me be compassionate. "I'm sorry, Mrs. Copley."

There was a long silence. "This is supposed to be fun." Kathy said eventually.

"Right," Dean agreed. "Let's have some fun, Mom. Copleys are really good at that."

Mrs. Copley rose from her throne. "Shall we go in to the dining room?"

They followed Mrs. Copley. Only the delicate clinking of silverware against china told her that there were other diners seated in the room. Despite the fact that it was a gloriously sunny day, the drapes were drawn, shrouding the room in shadows.

Kathy gave her a small smile. Her creamy skin, lustrous well-being and expensive clothes created a package of someone very well-off. But it was her jewelry that really made her look wealthy.

Lindsay had never seen so many glistening jewels on two hands, except for the time she and her parents had seen Liberace at the Warwick Summer Theater.

She wondered about the rings on her wedding finger, for if Kathy had a husband, he had not been mentioned yet.

From the highly polished hardwood floors to the early American originals gracing the walls, the dining room was the picture of propriety.

After ordering for them, Mrs. Copley monopolized the conversation, beginning with a complete history of the University.

She then launched into a diatribe against her best friend's son's new wife.

"Didn't know anything about planning a wedding, and believe me, it showed," she said with a disdainful sniff.

Dean looked at Kathy. "Didn't you go, too?"

Kathy looked confused. "I did. The weather was beautiful and things went off without a hitch."

"Lindsay, I hear you declined a business trip to London," Mrs. Copley probed.

"Yes, the timing wasn't right for me," Lindsay replied.

The waitress served their club sandwiches. As Kathy and Mrs. Copley began eating, Lindsay paused, saying her personal grace before meals.

"I'd never miss out on a trip to London!" Kathy said.

"Smells good, Mom." Dean bit into his cheeseburger.

"And most employers wouldn't be as indulgent as my son. There's Bobby Cichercia," Mrs. Copley said, nodding across the room.

The name sounded familiar to Lindsay. "The accountant?"

"The very one. He was in Ronald's class at Harvard. Unless you've been living under a rock for the past year, you'll know he's been in the news, on trial for that embezzlement case. Found him guilty, which I'm sure he was," she added derisively.

Lindsay picked at her meal. She didn't have much of an appetite, for some reason.

"No dessert for any of us, Daphne," Mrs. Copley told the waitress clearing their table. "Just the check."

Lindsay recognized Daphne from the Heart Association gala and gave her a friendly smile.

"This was very nice of you, Mrs. Copley. Thank you." Lindsay smiled.

"You're quite welcome." A smile cracked the scarlet slash that was her mouth. "You did so much on that dreadful day when my beloved husband was stricken."

"There's no one in the world like Lindsay." Dean looked at her affectionately.

"Quite true, I'm sure." Mrs. Copley turned to her but didn't say anything else.

"Let me take some pictures!" Kathy prompted. "Over here, by the fireplace." For once, Lindsay noticed, Kathy showed a genuine spark of life.

"I'll see you later. Kathy, meet me out by the car." Mrs. Copley swept from the room.

"Bye," they called.

Before Lindsay knew what was happening, Kathy was snapping away, flash bulbs brightening up the room.

"Kathy's a great photographer," Dean said, and Lindsay thought she heard pride in Dean's voice.

"She has a really nice camera. The fanciest I've ever used is one of those disposable ones from the grocery store."

"There's nothing wrong with those. They do a great job," Kathy said, snapping again. "I'll get you guys each a set of these," she promised. "I know they came out great."

Tucking her camera into her Coach shoulder bag, she gave Lindsay a quick hug.

"Nice to see you, Lindsay." Off she floated, in a swirling cloud of cashmere and Chanel No. 5 perfume.

Dean and Lindsay turned to each other.

"How you doing, Lindsay? Did you make it?"

"I don't know what to say." She waved her hand to indicate the opulence around her. "I told you before--I'm totally out of my league."

"No you're not, Lindsay. You're the kind of person who can fit in anywhere."

"I don't see myself in a place like this, or in quite that way."

He took her arm and they walked along the plush carpeting toward the exit. "Your father thought you were pretty special, didn't he?"

Lindsay nodded. "Yes." She spotted a powder room. "Let me stop here for a moment."

Dean nodded 'okay' and turned casually, appearing to examine some of the artwork adorning the walls.

She pushed open the heavy mahogany door and found herself in a lovely sitting room, with the lavatories in another area recessed beyond. The walls were covered in an apricot silk moiré, and a scrumptious cream-colored carpet muffled her footsteps. Lindsay thought it was the most beautiful room she had ever seen.

She could hear women's voices from the other side of the wall.

"She comes from nothing," one woman said disdainfully.

A chill ran up Lindsay's spine. The voice belonged to Mrs. Copley.

"And she's so common, Mummy," she heard Kathy say. "I think she actually believed me when I said I liked her gift! And what kind of a bumpkin would miss out on a trip to London?"

"Well, Dean is just going to have to move on. My son deserves someone like Gwynneth Holt. Someone with a pedigree. With social prominence. Someone sophisticated. Not someone in purple suede." Mrs. Copley made a noise of utter disgust.

Waves of nausea washed over Lindsay as she stood frozen in horror. What should she do?

"And my Dean deserves a woman who will devote herself to him full-time. Not someone who is really married to her mother. Calling him at the last minute. You saw what it did to your father and me. I won't have that happening to Dean. I won't. He deserves better."

Tears of humiliation and outrage splashed onto Lindsay's new suede vest.

"As if you can tell Dean what to do. You never could control him." Kathy gave a bitter laugh.

It made Lindsay sad to think of all the turmoil the Copleys had undergone. At the same time, she was tempted to defend her family to this woman...and tempted to confront her.

But she knew it would serve no good purpose. The best thing to do was to turn the other cheek. Not the easiest, but probably the best.

She'd remain invisible, and take heed of what she had overheard. At least she knew Dean was his own man, and not one to be swayed by any kind of outside pressure. Besides, they only worked together. There was nothing going on for Dean to "get over".

She backed out of the powder room and caught a glimpse of herself in a mirror just as Dean came around the corner to join her.

"You look like you've seen a ghost," he joked.

"It got a little stuffy in there," she fibbed. Casually smoothing her hair, she hoped her nervousness didn't show to him.

She had to hurry and get out of here before they came out of the ladies room. "Let's get some air." She grabbed Dean's arm with all her might and headed towards the door.

"I love it when you take charge," he said good-naturedly, helping her with her coat. "It's getting cold out there, you know. Are you sure you'll be okay at the football game?"

They walked along the brick sidewalk. Inhaling the crisp, fresh air, Lindsay thought about what had just happened.

"...very cold for November..." Dean was saying.

Her thoughts were jumbled. Maybe she wasn't enough of a "somebody" for Dean Singleton Copley. Maybe her working-class background was too humble for him, as he had been born into the American 'aristocracy'.

Was her home situation blinding her to the realities around her? Was she being selfish, spending time with him instead of her own family? After all, "charity begins at home" was a phrase she knew quite well. More importantly, though, why did she want to spend time with him? Her life was full enough. What was God's plan for her? When would she know?

"Mmmm." she replied absently. Her thoughts were clearing with each gulp of crisp, fresh air.

"So what are you going to do?"

Dean's question interrupted her thoughts. She realized she hadn't heard a word that he had said to her.

"About Thanksgiving?" he prompted.

"I'm sorry..."

"No problem, Lindsay. People often go into a trance after lunch with my mother."

She laughed.

"Thanksgiving?" he prompted again.

The thought of Thanksgiving without her father sobered Lindsay. "At first Meg didn't want to do anything this year. But we talked about it and we're going to carry on. Turkey and everything." She paused. "Meg and I are both sad and angry and scared. But we know we still have a lot to be thankful for. So I'm going to my church early to help set up with the meals they serve, then I'll be back home."

Dean's eyes widened. "You're serving at a soup kitchen on Thanksgiving? After all you've been through lately? Well, you know I was supposed to go to Palm Beach with everyone."

"Uh-huh. That sounds great."

"I'm not so sure it does, to me, any more. I'm thinking of staying here."

Lindsay raised her eyebrows. "Really? A cold New England Thanksgiving instead of a tropical holiday? Why?"

"There's a lot to do at work, and there won't be too many distractions."

"You can work when you get back. Don't you want to be with your family?" As soon as she said it, she realized that he probably didn't.

The look he gave her from the corner of his eye spoke volumes.

Lindsay's heartbeat quickened. "Why don't you come over to our house, then? But remember, it's not the Palm Beach Hilton," she added.

Dean put his arm around her shoulder. "It's better than that, in my eyes."

It seemed to Lindsay that the real Dean Copley was the type of man who knew what he liked, and what the rest of the world thought really wouldn't matter to him one bit. He knew his own mind, and he knew his own heart. She liked that side of him and would like to see more of it.

"I wouldn't want you disappointed, Dean. You know how grass roots we are. There won't be much of this." Sighing, she waved her hand to indicate their upscale surroundings.

There was a pause before Dean replied.

"Maybe not. But maybe for once I'll know what it's like to have a holiday celebration filled with all the things that money can't buy."

# *Chapter 10*

Despite the chilly November winds gusting outside, a standing room only crowd filed into Brown Stadium for the Bear's last home football game of the season against their archrivals, the Harvard Crimson.

As she carefully climbed up, up, up, the concrete stadium steps, Lindsay hoped her agitation from the terrible things she had overheard Dean's mother and sister saying about her in the restroom didn't show. Her mind was a tumult of emotions and she was only too glad to be holding tightly onto his sturdy, muscular arm.

Perhaps Mrs. Copley had a valid point. At first, Lindsay had thought she didn't really care what Dean's mother thought of her. But her reaction to what she had overheard in the lady's room told her that perhaps that wasn't true. Maybe she did care, more than she realized...because she cared for Dean. As did his mother, naturally. So they had something in common after all.

"Are we sitting with your family?" she asked.

He laughed. "Too rugged for them out here, Lindsay! They're in the box."

Relief flooded through her. *I should have known. The box.*

"But I like it out here," Dean continued, handing her a hot dog. "It's the real, pure football experience. Not the virtual one."

"I couldn't agree more." But deep down, Lindsay was wondering if she could really believe him. Could she? Coming from such a family of actors, how could she really know about his sincerity? She tried to push her doubts aside.

They settled onto their bench, huddled against the winds in the clear November sun. Lindsay noticed some dark clouds gathering on the horizon.

"You okay? Not too cold?" His eyes warmed when she gave him an enthusiastic nod as she finished her hot dog.

"Scrumptious," she managed to say.

Dean pointed to the corner of her mouth. "Mustard." Using his napkin, he dabbed it for her. "Seem like you're enjoying this more than that fancy stuff at the Ivy Club back there."

His hand was strong and gentle and warm. Lindsay remembered how tenderly he had cradled Claire's baby. It was endearing to see him be so careful.

"That's better." He smiled.

Their eyes met and Lindsay's heart skipped a beat. "I'm a down-home kind of girl," she answered.

His eyes twinkled. "Really?"

All she could manage was a nod. Lindsay didn't know what to say. She was so swept away by the moment, she almost didn't hear her cell phone ringing.

"Oh no," she fumbled in her purse.

All at once, the anxiety she lived with continually and the harsh reality of her home situation came right back to her, full force.

"It'll be okay," Dean reassured.

"Oh, I pray it will," she whispered.

She found the phone and flipped it open.

"Meg?"

"Lindsay." Meg was obviously troubled. "Where are you, honey?"

"We're at the football game." Lindsay could hear her mother's voice in the background. "How's Mom?"

"She's sundowning. I can't keep her still."

Lindsay caught Dean's eye. She hadn't had a chance to tell him about sundowning, the severe anxiety and agitation experienced by many Alzheimer's patients in the late afternoon, when the change in light and shadows turns a familiar room setting into a psychedelic fun-house. And since the afternoon had started to cloud over, it was getting dark even earlier than usual.

"That's okay, Meg. It's like we said. You've been through it before. We know to expect it."

"But I'm concerned she's going to put her fist through the window." Meg kept her voice low and modulated. She was in complete control.

Lindsay knew very well how incredible and worrisome it was to witness an Alzheimer's patient in the throes of a sundowning episode.

The disorientation, the yelling, the anxiety. Only a caregiver could recognize the symptoms and know that although it was an awful thing to see, it was a relatively harmless, and temporary, episode.

"Meg, I don't think she'll break the window. Can you distract her with some towels?" Like many Alzheimer patients, Mrs. Richardson became engrossed in folding the family's fluffy cotton towels. "She'll calm down as soon as it's dark." Out of the corner of her eye, Lindsay noticed a look of concern on Dean's face.

"She's all flushed and clammy."

"Meg, she's fine, believe me. Remember the article we read, about how it looks worse than it is? Sometimes it looks like the patient is going to have a heart attack.

"The main thing is having a lot of light in the house," Meg replied. "I'll pull the shades and put on all the lamps so it looks cozy in the house."

"Right. Give her the power drink, talk nice to her, sing, distract her. I'll be home by five."

"Thanks. Just please leave that phone on." A flash of the schoolmarm Meg emerged in her tone of voice, and then she sighed. "Poor Mom."

"I know, Meg. See you soon." After she clicked off Lindsay turned to Dean. "And such is the way it is."

Dean couldn't even imagine what it would be like to be involved in a situation like hers. His own mother always referred to her parents as a 'bane and a scourge' on her existence. He remembered one episode especially when he was younger and his grandfather had suffered a stroke the night before his family was slated to fly to the Caribbean.

After a few telephone calls lasting late into the night, past his bedtime, their vacation had gone on as planned. He realized, with no small sense of shame, he didn't even remember visiting his grandfather after they returned. Which was one reason why he didn't want to leave his father now.

It was hard for him to think about going through all the Richardsons had endured. And it was troublesome to think about what the future would hold for them. Yet, they seemed to draw strength from the very fact that they stuck together...and the very special love they shared. No matter how much heartache accompanied the closeness like the Richardsons shared, he knew the joy of their closeness would make it all worthwhile. How he wished he could experience that type of devotion. How he wished Lindsay would let him be a special part of her life.

He placed his hand gently on her arm. The look in his eyes was filled with caring and concern. But for once in his life, Dean Singleton Copley didn't know what to say.

Meg hung up the phone. Although she was happy her sister was able to get out, she had mixed feelings about Dean and all of Copley Industries.

*What would it all mean? Where was it all going?*

*I'm getting ahead of myself,* Meg thought.

It would be a bridge she'd have to cross when she got there. For now, there were more pressing issues. It occurred to her that there wasn't much sense in her being so mad with God. Things were happening anyway, and her anger wasn't helping her handle the situation more effectively. She had listened to the doctors and the scientists, read all the facts and the data. It still didn't seem to be enough. Could she do better if she listened to God?

For for the first time in a long, long while, Meg Richardson bowed her head and opened her heart to God in prayer.

Monday morning dawned bright and sunny, a direct contrast to Lindsay's gloomy state of mind. Yet she felt certain the decision she had made over the weekend was the only possible option for her.

All through the rest of the game on Saturday, Lindsay had been wondering what the future held for her. Dean explained all the plays to her, as excited as a college player, as animated as a professional sportscaster...but she had trouble keeping her mind on what he was telling her. Her thoughts kept wandering to home, and her mother's worsening condition. And when she returned home after the game, her concerns were proven to be right on target.

She couldn't kid herself, it was true her mother was declining. As much as she didn't want to believe it, the truth was staring her in the face. And, coupled with her deepening feelings for Dean had led her to the only possible decision: she was going to quit.

As she sat at her computer collecting her thoughts Monday morning and practicing what she was going to say, she also said a little prayer. *Please help me, Lord. I want to do the right thing.* But she wasn't getting the sense of serenity she usually felt after praying. There was something niggling at her heart, a sense she was running away from what God wanted from her. But surely He wanted her home, didn't He?

Why did Dean's smiling face keep creeping into her thoughts?

There was no possible way that God would want her with Dean...was there? How would she do that and take care of her mother, too? And what would God be thinking of, putting her and Dean together, when they were so obviously mismatched?

"Lindsay," As if her musings had come to life, Dean came into her office. She nearly choked on her coffee.

"You're making a career out of surprising me," she couldn't help but laugh.

Standing there, his eyes sparkling with life and vitality, he seemed to be everything strong and exciting that a man could ever be. Her heart skipped a beat.

Then the reality of what she was about to tell him came back to her, and her heart got heavy, knowing she was not being honest with herself. He wasn't going to miss having her working there, and she wasn't going to miss the job that much, either. She would miss the money, but she would manage somehow. It was Dean she was really going to miss.

Try as she might, she knew deep down in her heart of hearts she was running away from Copley Industries. Running away from her destiny. Running away from someone she might make happy. Running away from Dean. And from her Lord's will for her.

"What are you doing?" He came right over to her.

"Working on the day care proposal."

"Are you ready for a major news flash?"

She nodded in response and he continued.

"Good. I made a decision this weekend, and I've got you to thank for it. But that part comes later. Here's my announcement: I'm starting another business."

"What?" Lindsay blinked.

Dean paced the plush carpet excitedly.

"I'm sitting there, at the game with you on Saturday, and I'm thinking: 'There's more to life than money. And status.' I know there is! There's a thing called satisfaction. Fulfillment. A sense of contributing."

Lindsay listened, looking calm, heart pounding wildly.

"And I thought: how do I get this? Why don't I have it now? Then I realized, I don't ever really do anything for anyone but myself. My whole reason for being here at all is not even something I understand. I looked around me, and I tell you, Lindsay, it's as if a light went on. There I am at a football game. I've always loved sports. I loved those kids at Good Book Buddies. With my resources, why can't I start a nonprofit sports foundation for underprivileged kids? Let them learn about being team players, get fresh air and exercise, and give them something to aim for, some opportunities. Opportunities, that's all I've ever had."

"That's fantastic, Dean."

Nodding, he put his hand on his hips and his face became more somber.

"Yeah. Then I woke up."

"What do you mean?"

"I realized that there was no way that I could do it."

"Why not?"

After a long pause, he answered: "I can't let my family down. They need me here to run Copley Industries. I owe it to them." He shook his head. "Finally, my life has a purpose. I feel as if something is telling me this is what I should do. And I can't do it. I can't just go off and do something because it'll make me feel all warm and fuzzy. They're counting on me. And I'm not the type to let them down. God must be cruel to get His jollies by torturing people like me."

Lindsay rose from her desk quickly and sat beside him on the leather sofa. She placed her hand comfortingly on his arm.

"Oh, Dean, no. Don't say that. It's not like that at all."

He eyed her skeptically. "It feels like it is."

"God's ways aren't always clear to us. Sometimes that's very confusing. And yet, we have to trust Him. That's what faith is."

"It is confusing," he agreed, "What does God want us to do, then?"

"God guides our lives, Dean. He wants us to be happy. You'll know when you're on the right path." Her heart went out to him. She understood his turmoil. God had to let him know which direction was the right one. From what she could see, Dean wasn't selfish at all, despite what he thought about himself. But it wasn't her opinin that counted. It was how Dean felt about everything.

"Well how can I do this without letting my father down?"

She considered her words carefully before replying.

"I think you'll figure out a way, Dean, with faith, and trust. If your idea keeps coming into your mind and your heart, that's kind of like God telling you not to give up on it. Hang in there, and pray, and an answer will come to you."

"You think so? I'm not a big at praying. I don't know if I'm any good at it."

His innocence prompted her to smile. "I'm sure you're good at it, Dean Singleton Copley. Probably better than you think."

Some of his rakish charm returned. "I bet you say that to all the guys," he teased.

She shook her head.

"Thank you, Lindsay," he said softly. "I feel better. I don't know what's going to happen...maybe I can start the ball rolling slowly, or something..."

"That's a good idea," she said, then added, "And the camp is a great idea."

He rose from the sofa and headed for the door. "I'll keep you posted."

After he had gone, Lindsay slumped against the cool leather cushions. *I thought I was prepared for just about anything these days, Lord. But I wasn't expecting to fall in love with Dean.*

# Chapter 11

After Dean left her office, Lindsay grabbed the phone and dialed her friend Debbie's number in Phoenix.

"I know it's early, but..."

"Don't worry about it. I have to be in court early today, so I'm up. What's going on? I bet it's Dean."

She told Debbie about her feelings. Then she listened to the silence on the other end of the line. Eventually, Debbie spoke.

"Sure as a cactus plant has thorns, you're in love with this guy, Lindsay. And it sounds like you're laying one huge guilt trip on yourself about it."

"I am!" Lindsay wailed.

"You can't fight what you feel, Lindsay. It's not right. And we both know that Alzheimer's just advances, no matter who is there.

Don't delude yourself, Lindsay. Just say your prayers. God will guide you."

"Thanks, Deb. But these days, I'm not hearing much from God."

"No problem, you will. Remember that little thing called faith?"

"Yes..."

"Well? Now I'm going back to sleep."

Lindsay's thoughts darted all over the place after she hung up from Debbie. What shape would her mother really be in if she had been at home more instead of working? In all her time at Copley Industries, Lindsay had felt at home. It seemed like she belonged there. But at the expense of her mother? No way.

A few moments later Claire came in carrying cinnamon sticks and two steaming coffees, the morning tradition they had slipped into without formally setting it up.

"So how was your weekend?" Claire sat, eager to hear the details.

"Okay." Lindsay answered vaguely.

"Uh-oh. What's wrong?"

Lindsay knew it was the moment of truth. "I'm not going to be able to stay here, Claire. Working is too much for me."

Claire looked crestfallen. "You can't quit. You can't." Her voice was low.

Lindsay noticed Claire's reaction, hands shaking, which made her feel even worse, if that were possible.

"I don't want to, really, Claire. I feel so happy here. But my mother is declining." Although she thought she sounded convincing, she wasn't able to look Claire in the eye.

"But that's not your fault, Lindsay. It's the disease."

Lindsay couldn't answer. She knew Claire was right.

"You don't want Alzheimer's to claim you and Meg, though, do you? I've heard about the 'ripple effect' of this disease and that's what I worry about," she continued. "Your mother is a victim, no doubt. But I'm concerned that there may be more than one victim here if we're not careful."

"Me and Meg?"

"Exactly." She shook her head. "I think it's really admirable the way you gals are taking care of your mother." The look in her eyes was filled with caring and concern.

"Claire." Lindsay had a hard time speaking. "I...have to go..."

"Well, just think, Lindsay. Maybe it would be easier for you to go if it were the right decision." Claire's cheeks were pink and Lindsay knew she was upset. "Plus, there's another reason you shouldn't."

"What's that?"

"You know, ever since 'the accident' Dean has had trouble trusting anyone, especially himself, since he was the pilot and the crash was all his fault. I know it hasn't been long, but he's starting to trust you. Maybe you should trust him a little, too?"

"Claire, I just don't think I have time for that now. I have an obligation to my family to take care of."

The air in the room stood still.

"Well, if that's the way you feel...Good luck, dear." Giving Lindsay a warm clasp on her shoulder, Claire picked up her 'World's Greatest Grandma' coffee mug and left.

"Thank you for breakfast," Lindsay called after her.

Claire's answer a nod and a casual wave.

Lindsay held her head in her hands. Claire had been a good friend to her since her first minute here at Copley Industries. She would really miss working with her, but there was something else she had to do at the moment.

She made her way to Dean's office. *Lord, you're going to have to help me with this one.* Despite what Dean had said to her earlier, she still knocked at his door.

"What, Lindsay?" he called.

She entered his office and remembered her first visit to his office, not so long ago. Yet so many things had changed since then.

"Did you come for your cake plate?"

"Dean, we have to talk."

He approached her, carrying two remote controls. "It sounds serious."

She nodded.

"Did I make you feel awkward again?"

She shook her head, her heavy heart touched beyond words. "No, no. I'm thrilled about your new project. I'll help you as much as I can with it."

"I hope so. I know I'll need your help. You're the only reason I've even thought about it. I wouldn't really want to do it without you."

Lindsay closed her eyes. The hurt in her heart got worse. And the guilt on her shoulders was almost too much for her to carry. But she plunged on.

"The thing is, Dean, I'll have to help you from home. I can't keep working here. There's too much going on with my mother."

Dean's face fell. "What?"

"You'll have to find a new Administrative Assistant."

"I don't want one. I don't need one. I never did. Then you came along. And now I do need you."

Her pulse quickened from his words. And from the fib she was about to tell him. But at the last second, she knew she couldn't lie. "I was going to tell you that Melissa, the nurse, said my mother would do better if I were there." She took a deep breath. "But the truth is, I want to stay with her."

"It seems like you are very close," he replied. "I guess you have to do what you have to do."

"Thank you for understanding."

"I'm not sure I do. I asked you about this before you started."

Lindsay knew he was right. She looked at the floor. "Maybe when she's on a list to get placed in a home..."

After a moment, he said: "What about the day care project?"

"Gwynneth can handle that."

Dean scoffed. "No she can't."

"She can, but she doesn't care enough right now. Maybe that will change."

He followed her as she headed toward the door. "Don't go yet. Do me a favor?"

"What?" Her heart quickened.

"You're going to think this is the perfect proposal. Just stay for a week until Claire and I can get someone else? Please?"

The fact Dean didn't want her to leave meant more to her than Lindsay wanted to admit. Could she ever imagine that perhaps he loved her, too? What was going on with her?

Was it realistic to think she could control what was happening to her mother? Was the turmoil at her house just a smokescreen for her real feelings? Was Debbie right, after all? Was she hearing the real answer in her heart and just scared of all it meant? Was she running away from what God really wanted from her?

Questions swirled in her mind and in her heart. She was so confused! She rubbed her temples.

"And there's one more favor, too?" He raised his eyebrows.

"I'll try, Dean. What is it?" She didn't want to tell him he could always get a 'yes' from her.

"My father's getting out of the hospital today. Would you please come over and help welcome him home?"

Of course, this was the last thing in the world she wanted to do. After the humiliating things Mrs. Copley and Kathy had said about her in the ladies room, she really had all she could do to even think about seeing them again. She swallowed her pride and gave him a brave smile.

"What great news, Dean. I'll be glad to stop by. When should I get there?"

After she left his office, Dean peered through the glass panel of his office wall and watched what was going on. He saw her speak with Claire and things looked tense and uncomfortable. Usually, they'd be smiling or looking at each other. Not this time. Claire handed Lindsay a file, then Lindsay went into her office and closed the door.

*I've got to think of a way to keep her here!* Dean paced around his office, agitated and upset. *I'm not one for praying very much, Lord, but I'm asking for some inspiration now!*

They were standing outside his family's imposing brick mansion on one of the most prestigious streets in the state. The late afternoon sun sparkled across the snow-dusted lawn, making it shimmer like diamonds.

Lindsay chewed her lower lip. How could she act natural after overhearing what they really thought about her? Could she find it in her to be kind to them? It was all so awkward.

"I'm glad you could make it," Dean said with a smile. "I hope you're not nervous. There's no need to be."

"I'm doing okay. I'm really more nervous about my mother, to be honest with you. Have you advertised for a new assistant yet?"

He eyed her. "I'm not going to, Lindsay."

They entered the marble foyer and a uniformed maid hurried toward them.

"Mr. Copley, Madame," she said respectfully, taking their coats. "The family is having tea in the Rose Parlor."

Tea in the Rose Parlor? Lindsay gave Dean a wide-eyed stare, but he just shrugged.

It dawned on her then that perhaps he was nervous, or uncomfortable. After all, being with his family wasn't the easiest thing in the world for him. She had seen that at the Club.

Feeling like she was about to be presented to the Queen, Lindsay entered the Rose Parlor. The polite chatter ceased when she and Dean appeared in the doorway. Lindsay told herself to try and remember the real reason she was there--to welcome Mr. Copley home. That was truly a cause to give thanks.

"Dean, you're here!" Mrs. Copley swept over to them. "How are you Lindsay?"

"Fine, thank you," Lindsay answered politely.

"How's Dad?" Dean asked.

"He's feeling much better." As Mrs. Copley looked towards her husband across the room, Lindsay detected a tenderness and affection that she hadn't expected to find. Could she have been too harsh on Mrs. Copley?

Lindsay went over to where Mr. Copley was seated.

"Hello, Lindsay." Mr. Copley greeted her warmly.

"Welcome home. You look wonderful." She was relieved to see him in such good spirits.

"It's so nice to be home," Mr. Copley said. "Thank you for the flowers."

Dean joined them. "Dad!" He embraced his father carefully. Lindsay was glad to see them hug. Kathy and her husband Derek, as well as Dean's younger brother Fred and his girlfriend joined them and were introduced to Lindsay. It was all a blur.

"There are appetizers in the grand dining room now," Mrs. Copley announced. Then, to Lindsay's amazement, she took the handles of Mr. Copley's wheelchair and started pushing the chair.

On the way, Lindsay noted the expensive decor: huge glazed Oriental planters, gleaming marble floors, tapestry lining the walls, and statuary gracing the hallways.

And yet, there was a warmth in the air, a sense of the conversation being natural, which helped Lindsay feel at ease. She almost forgot she was in an elaborate mansion like the ones in Newport. It just felt like she was being welcomed into a family's private home.

"It's love that makes a house a home," she murmured.

"What?" Dean seemed confused.

They were seated at the long dining room table, which was adorned with silver candlesticks and fancy flower arrangements.

"Just thinking out loud," she answered. "I'm glad your father made it home."

She couldn't help but think about how lucky they were. Even though this homecoming was in different material surroundings from the kind her father would have been in when he came home from the hospital, she felt the happiness was just as deep. For the first time, she realized the sense of happiness that was something she had in common with the Copleys. Except that God had made other plans for her father.

Before she knew it, the visit had come to an end. Mr. Copley started to look tired.

"I hope you'll visit us again soon," Mrs. Copley said graciously.

"That's very nice of you, Mrs. Copley. Your home is beautiful and I can just imagine how happy you must be to have Mr. Copley back home and everyone here together."

Lindsay could have sworn she saw a tear glisten in the beautiful woman's eyes.

"Maybe we'll see you when we get back from Palm Beach," Kathy suggested.

Lindsay was confused.

"Are you able to travel so soon, Mr. Copley?"

He shook his head. "I'll be here for Thanksgiving."

"With me," Dean added.

They were leaving him? Lindsay could not understand why they would not be together for Thanksgiving. What she wouldn't have given to have her own father home. Yet, she thought, they must have their own reasons.

"Well, Mr. Copley," Lindsay said slowly, "I hope you like chestnut stuffing with your turkey dinner. It's a long-standing Richardson family recipe."

"I certainly do, dear," Mr. Copley patted her hands affectionately.

She did not miss the admiration in Dean's eyes when he looked at her. And Mrs. Copley was regarding her curiously.

"Thank you for a special time." Lindsay made a mental note to try and win her and Kathy over a little bit more after they returned from their trip. Maybe her first impression from the Ivy Club wasn't completely right. After all, because they would be out of town, she'd be seeing Mr. Copley and Dean. Maybe God had sent someone her way to ease the pain a little.

Dean walked her to her car. "That wasn't too awful." His tone was dry.

"Not at all. They were lovely and I had a very nice time. Thank you."

"They're pretty predictable, but basically harmless."

Lindsay's heart went out to him. It couldn't be easy, having had his own huge loss to cope with. "They love you, Dean. It was nice of them to include me in this welcoming get-together for your father. And I'm sure they all had a million other things to do."

"That's kind of the problem, though."

"I know. But they are here, with you."

Images of her own family in better times flooded through her mind. What she wouldn't give to have them all together again. Maybe that's how the Copleys felt sometimes, too.

"Thanks for stopping by," Dean said.

"No problem. See you tomorrow." After they said good-bye, Lindsay could hardly wait to get home and see Meg and her mother. Just as she hoped, Meg met her at the door with a warm hug.

"Aunt Charlotte heard of a last-minute opening at a local nursing home, so she and I are going out tomorrow afternoon when Melissa is here. We'd love for you to come, Lindsay, but you're working and time is of the essence. You understand, don't you?"

"Sure." Lindsay gave Meg a sunny smile, even though she was a little disappointed. "It's all about doing what is best for Mom."

# *Chapter 12*

"Let's read the story of Jacob and Esau!" little Matthew Graham cried, eager to start his Good Book Buddy session with Lindsay the next day.

"That's a good one, Matthew. Can you tell me the moral of the story?"

"Lying is bad," Matthew answered simply. "God wants us to always tell the truth."

A lump formed in Lindsay's throat. She glanced over at Dean and Claire, engrossed in their readings, too. Both of them meant so much to Lindsay after such a short time. Maybe Claire had a point. Was she giving things enough of a chance? Could she be running away?

The Awards for Athletic Excellence Banquet began at eight PM that evening, with a social hour starting at seven. Dean didn't begrudge going in his father's place; like Lindsay had felt, he, too, was proud to represent his father. But he was not looking forward to arriving with Gwynneth on his arm. And no doubt his friend Gordon would give him no end of grief about showing up with Gwynneth. Easy for him, the happily married man. No idea whatsoever what life as a bachelor was all about. Or what life with a Gwynneth would be either.

Why had his mother sent Gwynneth into his office in a last-minute panic? Or had she, really? Perhaps it was all Gwynneth's doings. He had told her repeatedly that they did not have a future together, but she always refused to take him seriously.

And this evening proved to be no exception. All through dinner she was posturing, posing, and acting as if she were his wife. She made sure to be draped all over him every time Mike went to snap a shot.

He could barely stand himself for living a lie. He should not have gone along with taking Gwynneth. Lindsay was the one he wanted, and it was time to tell her so.

Lindsay was reviewing some information on newly printed spreadsheets when Dean came into her office the next morning.

"Hi, Dean," she smiled. "What's up?"

He sat, heels up on her desk. "Not much. How's everything at home? With your mother?"

"Well, Dean, I wanted to speak with you about that." She knew it was time for her to admit the truth to him. She straightened the bun coiled at the base of her neck.

"You might not know this, but one of the many Boards I'm on is the NHA --"

"The Nursing Home Association." Her heart leapt. *Could he help them?*

"I've been concerned about you Richardsons, so I made a few calls late yesterday to see if I could help out. Sometimes that happens, when someone has a little pull, they can move someone's name up on the list and get them placed sooner. Follow me?"

Nodding, Lindsay gave him a hopeful smile. "And?"

"It's not going to take long to place your mother, Lindsay. There are rooms available nearly everywhere, just say the word. You won't have a long time with her at home." He moved closer to her. "You don't really have to leave here."

"I was going to tell you." Her voice was small.

"What were you going to say?"

"This isn't easy for me, Dean." Her voice faltered. She looked down at the desk and sighed. With all the gumption she could summon up, she looked at him squarely and told him the truth.

"I said my mother was the reason I have to leave. In my heart I meant it. Except it wasn't really for her. I see now. The reason was because I was scared of what I'm really feeling. And being scared is the real reason I wanted to go."

"But you know things will work out at home." Dean looked puzzled.

"Actually, I'm not really worried about home all that much. I wish it didn't have to change. But I know it does."

"So what are you so scared of?"

She rolled her eyes in exasperation. Was he thick in the head? Couldn't he see? Then she remembered, he wasn't "touchy-feeley". She pressed on, and declared: "It's you! I'm starting to feel really close to you. Like maybe I'm getting too close. And want to get even closer."

He seemed stunned. "You have feelings for me?"

She nodded. "Yes, I do. But it's just so selfish. Our worlds are too different. And I'm embarrassed...and then working together..."

A smile spread across his face. "I can't believe it, Lindsay, this is wonderful."

"I wanted to tell you the truth..."

"You can't run away from life. Or from what God wants for you." His voice was gentle.

Her mouth fell open in astonishment, then she felt shy and unsure. She buried her head in her hands. "I'm sorry," she murmured. "But how can God be calling me in two directions at the same time?"

Dean eyed her quizzically. "I don't follow."

"Honestly, I do feel like I need to take care of my mother. It's one of the Ten Commandments. And yet, here you are...this nice job...your father..."

They walked over to the love seat and sat down.

Dean never stopped looking at her. "The last thing in the world I want is to lose you, Lindsay. I know I need some brushing up on my Scripture, but as I recall the very first commandment goes something like this: 'I am the Lord, thy God. Thou shalt not have strange gods before me.'"

Lindsay nodded. "Pretty good. But what do you mean?"

"We can all interpret that lots of different ways --"

"People set up money as their god - "

"Exactly." Dean looked at her thoughtfully. "But it's also other things. Character traits, for instance. Maybe it comes down to being all about putting our will, what we want, first as a 'strange god', before what God wants for us."

Dean's words sank into her consciousness and she sucked in her breath. "Maybe I'm proud? Maybe I'm wrong? Maybe I'm fighting what God wants for me?"

"Without meaning to, maybe you are." He reached out to take her hand. "Maybe God is showing you what your life path is supposed to be now. Taking care of your mother, was good, Lindsay. You did all you could." He placed his index finger under her chin and tilted her head back. "Maybe now it's time for you to see the future God has in store for you. Whatever it is."

Thoughts and emotions swirled chaotically in Lindsay's head. Could she be hearing him right? "I was so scared before. And now I don't feel one bit scared at all."

"Sometimes it takes courage for us to face the future God had planned for us," he added. "I think they call that faith."

"Something is telling me that you are so right, Dean. But it's been so scary to think of how things are changing so quickly. I'll never get this time with my mother back."

"No, you won't. But we'll all be here. And we can face whatever we need to, together. We're the Copley Team."

"But you were so mad at me before, when I missed that meeting."

"I'm not perfect. And I'm not saying I won't get mad again, but I got mad because I care. And I know a little more about the situation now. There is that little virtue called 'trust' hanging around, you know. You might want to use some of it in this instance." He raised his eyebrows.

She sighed. "So I probably don't have to leave my job here."

He shook his head. "Very good, because your mother is one of my favorite people and I want to keep up on her."

"And you know you're one of her favorites." She sighed again. "Claire was so right."

Dean shrugged. "She usually is."

"I felt so awful, I hope she'll forgive me." She drew her brows together in confusion. "Say, tell me: when did you get to be such an expert in scripture interpretation?"

"I don't know. Since I met you, it seems to be coming back out of my subconscious faster than I can spout off about it."

"It's certainly going to make for a nice Thanksgiving," she murmured.

"Try and get some work done now." His tone was wry. "It would be a nice change."

Lindsay felt emotionally exhausted when he left. It took a few rings of her cell phone to call her back to reality. She answered it, and heard Meg's voice on the other end.

"Lindsay, I'm at Greendale Glen with Aunt Charlotte and it's beautiful here." Meg spoke gently.

"Greendale Glen?"

"It's a home here in Bristol. Lindsay, I've just completed the paperwork." Meg continued without hesitating. "Thanks to Aunt Charlotte's pull and influence, they've accepted Mom on the list. And they'll have a bed ready for her next Monday."

On his way back to his office, Dean watched Lindsay through a glass panel. She was holding her cell phone away from her face and wiping tears from her eyes. What could she be crying about?

Then she went over to Claire, and after speaking briefly, the two hugged like long-lost sisters. Something tugged at Dean's heart. And something told him that the days might be over when all he'd ever be in life was an observer to such genuine and sincere closeness. Incredible.

Lindsay was so preoccupied with these recent developments after she spoke with Claire that she nearly walked head-on into Gwynneth in the corridor. She thought Gwynneth looked like a snake in her tight-fitting python print jumpsuit. Then she remembered she was at work and supposed to be working.

"I'm sorry, Gwynneth!"

"Right," Gwynneth replied.

"Gwynneth, why don't we get together and get going on that day care project? Time's slipping by fast."

"That's because you're the one who's never available, not me. Let's get started right now."

"Okay." Lindsay followed Gwynneth into her office, admiring the mauve and cranberry decor. "Where are the plans?"

"We don't have any yet, thanks to you. I want to talk to you about something else. It won't take long."

"What is it?"

"I was just wondering how far you're planning to carry this little charade."

"Excuse me?"

Gwynneth flipped her hair over her shoulder. "Cut it out, Lindsay. Don't pull that innocent routine with me. You must know I'm in on every trick in the book."

"I don't know what you're talking about, Gwynneth. And you must know, I'm really busy."

"So you're not going to make this easy. Fine. As you wish." She walked over to the windows. "In case you don't know it, Dean is mine."

It was Lindsay's turn to roll her eyes. "Right, Gwynneth. You told me."

"But didn't it sink in? It seems..."

An idea struck Lindsay. "You must have arranged for Mike to get your picture with him there. You're waging your own publicity campaign."

"I'm sure no one's ever accused you of being too sharp."

Lindsay ignored the dig. "Don't you know Dean better than that? He'll never do anything just to satisfy popular opinion. How pathetic of you."

Lindsay's heart was suddenly filled with pity for this poor, misguided beauty. She reached out to her.

"Gwynneth." Lindsay used her gentlest tone. "You're too young to carry all this fury and this bitterness. You must realize there are some things in life that we can't control, we're not meant to control. If you don't feel that Dean is into you the way he should be, maybe it says more about him than it does about you."

"What do you mean?"

"Well, you're beautiful, wealthy, socially prominent...maybe there's another reason why Dean isn't really yours."

"No one said he isn't," she scoffed. "But like what?"

Lindsay shrugged. "I don't know; but I'd look inside myself. Within. Maybe you're just used to thinking about him as yours, but what's in your heart?"

Gwynneth looked at her as if she had just sprouted another head.

Lindsay forged on, remembering her talk with Dean. "Lots of times we do what's expected of us, or what we think is expected...and when it doesn't turn out right, we're confused. But the reason was with us all along--we didn't see what God expected of us, or meant for us." Reflecting on her words, Lindsay couldn't believe she hadn't seen this sooner. Thank God for Dean's kindness and compassion, and the way he had spoken to her about it.

"God? Oh, come on." Gwynneth backed away.

"It's true. Please, Gwynneth, please think about coming with me to my Bible study group. It helps when you're trying to look within. Or work on the penny social with me and Claire."

Gwynneth laughed, jeeringly. "Penny social? You can't be serious!" Her eyes hardened into a steely cold glint. "And let me tell you something, Little Miss Church Lady. You think Dean Singleton Copley is a Boy Scout. Well he's not. There's a lot about him that you don't know. A lot."

"Gwynneth, just think about..." Lindsay tried one more time.

"Just get out of here. And remember, no matter what you do on this stupid project, I'm going to be doing all I can to make you look bad." Her voice was low as she slammed the door. Lindsay walked thoughtfully down the hall.

# *Chapter 13*

Lindsay was standing in line at Garden Terrace Florists around the corner from work later in the afternoon. With all that was going on, she was very glad she had remembered Claire's birthday was the next day.

"Yes?" The well-dressed clerk said.

Lindsay introduced herself and explained why she was there. "Claire has been a good friend to me from the minute I arrived at Copley Industries."

The clerk brightened right away when she heard Claire's name.

"I'm Fatima," she shook Lindsay's hand cordially. "We'll be happy to handle everything for you. Claire is such a dear."

"That she is." Lindsay remembered how good it felt when they had made up after she told Claire that she was staying.

She reviewed her mental list of what she needed for Claire's party: a card had already been circulated and signed by everyone, the gift certificate to a local spa for a day of beauty had arrived, she would take care of refreshments and a cake, and the musicians from her church were all lined up; Gwynneth, Cassidy and Belinda, Mrs. Copley, Kathy and other Copley employees were all planning to attend. Of course, Dean would be there right after his meeting. She couldn't think of any loose ends.

"...was such a tragedy," the clerk was saying.

"Sorry?"

"I was just reminiscing about how awful the accident was."

Lindsay looked confused.

Fatima lowered her voice. "You know, when Claire lost her husband in Vail."

Lindsay's stomach lurched. "Twelve years ago? In the helicopter?"

Fatima nodded. "And she's still loyal to those Copleys. I don't know how she does it."

"She's remarkable," Lindsay managed as she signed the receipt Fatima placed before her. *Bless you, Claire,* Lindsay thought. Having a friend like Claire was another reason why she was glad she was staying at Copley Industries.

"Surprise!" Everyone called when Claire came back from lunch the following day.

Claire turned beet red and Lindsay snapped a quick picture.

"You're not turning into Mike, are you?" Dean quipped.

"I'm selling them to The Register." Lindsay laughed.

Belinda held Cassidy, who squealed to the delight of everyone around her.

The bright November sun streamed into the reception area, and the string quartet played softly in the corner.

Mrs. Copley caught Lindsay's eye once and gave her a polite smile. Mr. Copley, however, gave her a warm hug. Lindsay was glad to see he was out of his wheelchair.

"How nice of you to arrange this, dear. Claire is one of our closest personal friends and dearest employees." His voice was warm.

"I can see why. She's even helping out with the penny social at our church."

"Really?"

Lindsay nodded. "And Dean has donated lots of items, too, from Copley Industries."

Mr. Copley smiled. "That's what I wanted to speak with you about, Lindsay."

Lindsay looked at him expectantly. "Yes?"

"I know he feels he has to stay here," he said, "but I hope someday he'll realize that we really don't expect it of him. Maybe you will help him see the truth."

"It's going to take time." Lindsay was thoughtful, imagining just what it must be like for Dean, and for his father, too. "He still has a lot of issues with everything that happened and he doesn't want to let any of you down."

"You know all this?" Mrs. Copley asked.

"He told me at the hospital," Lindsay answered. "In fact, he's amazed all of you even speak with him...and he doesn't think he deserves your love."

"We couldn't love him more if we tried." Mrs. Copley's voice choked with emotion.

"How true, how true," Mr. Copley agreed.

Lindsay was touched by their obvious affection for Dean. *When would he see it?*

"And how are you feeling, Mr. Copley?" she asked.

"I'm fit as a fiddle and looking forward to Thanksgiving at your house, my dear."

"Me, too." Lindsay was still amazed that the other Copleys were going out of town, but didn't mention it to him.

"I'm thinking about staying in town," Mrs. Copley said.

"That would be nice. If you're here, you're more than welcome to come over."

Mrs. Copley gave Lindsay a curious look. "Thank you."

The group sang 'Happy Birthday' to Claire, and after she sliced her cake, Lindsay took an extra piece to Dean's office for him to have after the party. She smiled as she heard him leading another chorus of 'Happy Birthday' to the group as she hurried down the hall to his office.

*I bet he'll enjoy this later*, she thought. Scuttling across the plush carpet, she was just about to place the dish on his desk when her heel snagged in the pile of the carpeting and she went flying, face-forward, in an Olympic style swan dive. She was only able to brace herself at the edge of his now cake-covered desk.

"Oh, great," she groaned. "What a mess." She cringed as she viewed the chocolate and the fork and the icing gob strewn across Dean's piles of papers. "I am too clumsy to live!"

Snatching a wastebasket, she started scooping the mess off of his desk using the soiled file folders. She was peering across the top of his desk when Kathy walked in.

"What are you doing?" she asked. "Why are you alone in Dean's office, holding his confidential files?"

"Oh, Kathy, I'm such a klutz," Lindsay stammered. "I wanted to leave an extra piece of cake on Dean's desk for later but I tripped and fell! Believe me, I was planning to keep it on the plate." She shrugged. "It's the truth."

Kathy's eyes narrowed. "I think you're snooping. I'm calling security."

Lindsay's eyes went round. "There's cake all over me!"

Just then, Gwynneth appeared. "What's going on in here, Kat?"

"You won't believe it, Gwynneth. I found her here, snooping around Dean's desk."

"I've seen her do that before, too," Gwynneth said, nodding.

"And then," Kathy continued, "when I walked in on her, she smeared the cake all over herself to make it look like she wasn't spying."

"Kathy! How can you lie about me? And why?" Lindsay was aghast.

"Call Security." Gwynneth advised and Lindsay thought she saw a glint of satisfaction in her made-up eyes.

Before anyone could move, the harpist poked her head in. "There you are, Lindsay. Our time is about up."

"What's going on, did the party move in here?" Dean said in a good-natured tone from the hall as he entered the office, holding Cassidy comfortably in his arms.

He took one look at the frozen tableau and his smiling expression disappeared. Taking an envelope out of his pocket, he handed it to the harpist, along with Cassidy.

"Take the baby back to Claire for me, please? And you did a nice job," he commented. She vanished down the hall.

"She's snooping through your files." Gwynneth said dramatically.

"Dean." Both Lindsay and Kathy spoke at the same time.

"Kathy thinks I'm a spy and a security risk."

Dean glanced from one to the other. Then his gaze settled on Lindsay. "You're a *dry cleaning* risk, that's for sure."

Lindsay thought she saw the corners of his mouth twitch, but she was too upset to really think about it.

Kathy was whiter than usual. "This isn't funny, Dean."

"She's looking through your files," Gwynneth repeated.

Dean took two steps into the office. "This is worse than the second grade. Gwynneth, go."

"But Dean - "

He silenced her with a look. She scuttled out and Dean quickly closed the door. Lindsay had never seen such a look in his eye. He seemed disheartened and upset at the same time. For some crazy reason, it came into her head at that moment how much her father would have liked Dean.

Handing Lindsay his handkerchief, he commented: "Another one bites the dust."

"Yup." Lindsay nearly choked on the sobs of outrage and humiliation in her throat.

"Kathy, apologize to Lindsay."

"But I - "

"Now."

There was a pause and Lindsay said a quick prayer for peace.

"No, I won't, Dean. She doesn't deserve it." Kathy sounded like a child.

"I won't hear you speak ill of her, Kathy."

"Maybe you won't but Mummy will. And so will Daddy."

"Please..." Lindsay said, but was silenced by a look from Dean.

"Daddy has enough trouble, Kathy. You'd better not add to it with one of your jealous, irrational tirades."

"I won't. You'll be sorry for this, Dean." She glared at Lindsay and continued. "You'll be sorry, too. We all know what you're like. Gwynneth sees it. Mike sees it, too. Everyone sees it but Dean."

"That's quite enough, Kathy," he warned.

"I'm only starting."

Dean approached her. "If you don't apologize now, we won't be able to repair this damage."

Kathy looked at Dean, then at Lindsay. Her eyes narrowed. "You'll never get me to apologize."

"Well then I will, Kathy," Lindsay broke in earnestly. "There's no need for any of us to harbor bad feelings. I don't want to cause a rift between you and your brother. Family is too important. Please accept my apologies."

But Kathy just looked at her.

Lindsay continued. "I don't have any hidden agenda against you, Kathy, or Copley Industries. I'll a take lie detector test if you want me too. Come on. Please?" She moved to embrace Kathy, who stepped aside.

"You're both so stupid, you can drop dead for all I care." She turned on her high heels and walked out of the room.

"Kathy, wait." Lindsay moved to follow her, but Dean held her arm. "Let me go, Dean! I want to settle this."

"Don't bother, Lindsay." His tone of voice stopped her. "This has been smoldering for a long time. Just let nature take its course here. And let me settle my family scores."

She knew it wasn't her place to pursue it. "But I want to help," she said, knowing she was defeated.

"Your time will come, Lindsay." He took her elbow and opened the door. "For now we have guests to entertain."

"No, I can't, Dean. Not with all this dissension."

Dean scoffed. "This is nothing. You should see it when the Copleys get going."

"It's awful!"

"It's the way it is."

"But Kathy is your sister." Lindsay could never in her wildest dreams imagine having a scene with Meg that came anywhere near the awful exchange she had just witnessed.

"She can take it or leave it." Dean shrugged. But Lindsay noticed he did not look her in the eye.

"There it is again, the mask." Lindsay said. "I thought you were getting past that, Dean."

"What are you talking about?" His tone was cool. "Come on, we have party guests."

Lindsay felt the color rising to her cheeks. "Life isn't all parties at the Club and evening soirees at swanky hotels, Dean. Life is all about love, and sacrificing for those you love. It's about service, and..."

"That's enough." Dean's voice was barely audible. "Get off your bully pulpit, Lindsay Richardson. I don't need a sermon from you or anyone in this world about sacrifice and service. Remember what happened to my brother?"

"That's what I mean."

He looked puzzled and she continued. "Don't hide from your true feelings, Dean. Don't hide from life, or from God."

"I'm not," he answered, stuffing his fists in his pockets.

"Maybe not. Wouldn't you want to go find Kathy and make things right?" Her voice choked, but she continued. "All the gifts you have been blessed with, and you seem to think..."

She couldn't finish because she began to feel waves of nausea sweep over her. "People who have the kinds of blessings you have are on their knees thanking God every night."

"How do you know I don't do that, Lindsay?" he challenged.

She shook her head and left the office, a righteous hiccup escaping just before she closed the door.

But how come she had a nagging feeling that maybe Dean had a point?

Lindsay was sick at heart all night. First thing in the morning, she called her pastor, Fr. Marchand.

"Of course, dear, I'll see you right after early Mass," he agreed.

"I won't keep you long, Father," she promised.

Seated in St. Gregory's Rectory the following morning, she replayed the scene from the previous day over and over in her mind.

Was she wrong to tell Dean how she felt? Had she spoken out of turn? Was it her place to get involved in family issues? As employee, as friend...what was her role in Dean's life? Was she pushing too hard?

She smoothed the pleats on her royal blue paisley skirt, and straightened the matching jacket and scarf. Her heart beating frenetically, she waited for Fr. Marchand to appear.

Slender rays of winter sun filtered through the French windows in the parlor. Through them, she could see the two-storied brick elementary school across the street. How were her students doing? It seemed like a lifetime ago when she had been there.

Muffled footsteps crossing the well-worn carpet in the hallway gave her notice of Fr. Marchand's approach.

"Lindsay. How are you, my dear?" The sixty-five year-old pastor welcomed her robustly.

She rose to greet him. "Good morning, Father. Thank you so much for seeing me."

Lindsay thought that if ever an individual was perfectly suited to his occupation, it was Fr. Marchand. Even though his hair was a white as snow, and his face creased from years of ministering, his voice and his bearing were those of a man twenty years his junior.

He shook her hand warmly, and motioned her to sit down. "So tell me what's on your mind, my dear." He peered at her gently through his wire-rimmed glasses.

She sighed. "I'm torn and confused, Father."

"About what?"

Lindsay proceeded to fill him in on the recent developments in her life. Losing her father, her mother's condition, her new job, her feelings for Dean...all the twists and turns of her circumstances came tumbling out as she tried to explain her torment.

"So how do I reconcile these two opposite directions, Father? How do I let someone else take care of my mother? How do I know if I have a future with Dean? How do I know what God wants me to do?"

Fr. Marchand looked thoughtful for a minute, then spoke, choosing his words with care.

"You know that the good Lord wants all of us to be happy, Lindsay, and to go in faith to love and to serve Him."

"Uh-huh," she urged him on. She needed answers.

"I think you must look in your heart and find the way, in your life now, that you will best serve the Lord. Is it in keeping on insisting that you'll be your mother's primary caregiver, even though she will soon be placed in a home? Or is it in letting her go, and finding the courage to face the future God has prepared for you?"

Lindsay knew the answer right away. She looked down at her hands, folded in her lap. This wasn't the answer that she wanted to hear.

"It's not that easy to let her go, Father."

"For her own good?"

She looked at him, remembering her conversation with Dean.

*'I never would have been that casual about losing my job,' he had said. 'I would have raised the roof to save my job...'*

*'Do you think that you would do that at your mother's expense, Dean?' she had asked.*

Yet isn't that exactly what she was thinking of doing now, she wondered, her thoughts returning to the present. How smug she had been! But she nearly missed the chance to see her own situation with truth and humility.

"We have a phrase, Lindsay, that I'm sure you know." Fr. Marchand said.

"What is it?"

"Let go, and let God."

"Let go and let God," she repeated. The meaning of the phrase sank in. Trust in the Lord, completely. No one ever said it was going to be easy, though. But she knew it was just what she had to do.

"Thank you, Father." She stood to leave. "I'm so sorry."

He gave her a caring hug. "Good luck to you, Lindsay. And God bless you."

# *Chapter 14*

Dean maneuvered one of the Copley Industries service vans through the early evening traffic. The trip from Providence hadn't taken even twenty minutes. With a little luck, he'd be back at home just in time to enjoy tonight's prime time football game on his sofa.

Turning carefully into the parking lot of St. Gregory's church, he peered through the darkness to find the delivery entrance to the church hall. One dim light bulb was all he could discern.

*This place could use some beefed up security, and lighting,* he thought. *I wonder how their heating system is? Not great, I bet.*

He was still thinking about his exchange with Lindsay the day before. She really made him think. As it turned out, he had a seminar to attend in Boston all day and hadn't even been to the office today. He smiled as he thought of her, warming at the image of her smile.

*Wouldn't it be nice if she were here?* he thought, backing up to the service entrance.

Hopping out of the van, he banged on the back door. After a moment, it was opened by a wiry man of about seventy, with a huge ring of keys dangling from his well-worn leather belt.

"I'm Dean, with the stuff for the penny social. You must be Salty. Lindsay told me about you."

With a tip of his head, the man answered: "You're early."

Dean opened the van doors. "I never cut things too close, Salty. Gets on my nerves. If there's one thing I can't stand, it's having a change in my plans at the last minute." He stacked some boxes on the driveway. "Know what I mean?"

"Nep."

Dean couldn't tell if that was a yes or a no, but decided to let it go. "Watch that stack, there, Salty. Those can get heavy."

"What's going on here?" a shrill voice cried.

"Just unloading for the penny social," Dean answered.

"Keep yer shirt on, Mrs. Cabral!" Salty yelled, then spouted a laugh that turned into a hacking cough.

"Get back in here, Salty! You need to change!"

Salty ignored her screeching, attacking the heavy stack with renewed gusto. Dean was immersed in his own work until he heard an unusual grunt from Salty.

Looking over, he saw his new friend bent in half, hands clutching his lower back. He looked up at Dean, who thought he saw a glint of mischief in Salty's beady eyes.

"Salty, are you okay?" Dean offered his hand.

"Threw my back out," he answered.

Mrs. Cabral bustled over to them, wringing her hands. "I knew something was going to happen! What a catastrophe! Salty, you've really done it this time!"

"Well, I don't think he did it on purpose," Dean said.

"What do you mean? He's hurt, and now I need to find another Santa!" she cried.

If the earth could have opened up in that instant and swallowed him whole, Dean truly wouldn't have minded. What was going to happen next flashed before him in his mind's eye. And sure enough, just a beat behind, Mrs. Cabral came up with the same idea.

"You're going to have to fill in for him as Santa," she stated.

Dean shook his head, and backed away from her. "Oh no, I don't think so. That's not an option."

"What else am I going to do?" Mrs. Cabral wailed. "Why can't you?"

*I have a million and one reasons,* he thought, taking a deep breath of the crisp night air. And all of a sudden not one of them seems any good!

A slow smile curved his lips. Lindsay would really love this, wouldn't she? "There's no reason why I can't help you out, Mrs. Cabral," he finally said.

"That's the Christmas spirit," Salty said, then broke into another coughing fit.

A total of twenty-eight volunteers were stationed at the twelve decorated booths in the wood-paneled basement of Lindsay's church for their annual Holiday Penny Social.

"I can't believe these lovely cactus plants your friend Deborah sent."

Claire's cheeks were pink with excitement as she removed the plants gently from their shipping cartons and stuck price tags carefully on each one.

"She's fantastic. And as soon as she finishes law school she'll be moving back to Rhode Island to practice. Then watch out." Lindsay smiled proudly.

"I can't wait to meet her." All of a sudden, Claire's mouth dropped open in astonishment. "That's not Salty, he's too tall. Who's playing Santa?"

Lindsay turned to the main entrance. Someone dressed as Santa was making his way through the crowd. "Ho, ho, ho," he bellowed, "where's my chair?"

Lindsay recognized his voice. "It's Dean!"

She and Claire burst into peals of laughter as he moved towards the oversized red velvet chair next to an artificial fireplace in the corner of the room that bore a sign: "Santa's Corner."

"Let's hear from the children!" he cried.

"I guess he forgot it doesn't start for another half hour," Claire said dryly, prompting them to another round of laughter. Lindsay wiped the tears from her eyes and walked over to him.

"Yes my dear?" He patted his lap, playing the part expertly. "If you say one word, you're fired," he added in a husky stage whisper.

"I'll try." She stifled a giggle. "I can't believe this, Dean. Is that really you?"

"Yes. And what's so strange about it?"

"Well, you told me you'd never be Santa."

"Well I didn't know Salty when I said that. And I didn't know he had a bad back."

"That is so great of you, Dean," Lindsay beamed.

"That smile is a nice gift." Dean eyed her intently from behind his big white beard and shaggy wig. "But I'm used to material gifts, like the things I brought here." He indicated several box loads of gifts alongside the wall.

"Oh Dean, thank you. You're going to make this the best penny social ever."

"I wanted to help, but I never thought I'd be Santa."

"Sometimes God has other plans for us, remember?" she said, "to quote you..."

"Excuse me?" Mrs. Cabral interrupted them.

"Hi, Mrs. Cabral. Have you met Santa?"

Pursing her lips, Mrs. Cabral looked at them askance. "Lindsay, shouldn't you be setting up your floral display? Really, Santa is here for the children."

"I guess that's my cue to exit," Lindsay replied good-naturedly.

"Now, is that the Christmas spirit?" Dean raised his bushy eyebrows.

"You can socialize with Santa later, if you really must," Mrs. Cabral added, rolling her eyes as Lindsay hurried over to the used book table.

"How's Salty?" Dean asked.

"He's fine," Mrs. Cabral answered.

"I may be playing Santa, but I know when things are tense. What's bothering you, Mrs. Cabral?"

"Lindsay has brought a lot of publicity to us here through her association with you, Mr. Copley. And we're not so sure we welcome all that outside interest. It takes away from our reverence."

"Outside stuff can't do it to you. You do it to yourself. I'm a businessman. I know." Dean spread his hands, palms up, in the air. "And it might pay off for you."

"How so?"

"If there's a lot of interest, there may be more people here and that means..."

"More money." Mrs. Cabral smoothed her apron. "I hadn't though of that."

"You might want to ponder it. I told everyone I know to come here tonight."

Her eyes widened. "Did you want a receipt for that merchandise, Mr. Copley?"

"That would be nice."

"I'll be sure you get one."

He watched her leave, then motioned Lindsay back towards him.

"Lindsay, I may be a newcomer, but isn't there some phrase like 'charity begins at home'?"

She sighed. "Sure is. Some folks do it when it comes easily, for something like this. But when the connections are a bit more abstract it's a little harder for them." She shrugged.

"We might have to see what we can do about changing that mentality," Dean said thoughtfully. The people piled in to the bazaar he noticed and the crowd grew in numbers. Which meant more money for the church. "In the meantime..."

He reached for his cell phone. "Now what?" she asked, barely able to wait to see what Dean was concocting.

After three rings, Mike was able to pull the phone across the coffee table by the cord and grab the receiver.

"Yup," he mumbled, rubbing his eyes with the base of his palm.

"What took so long? Are you sick?"

"No, Dean. I'm just not a type-A personality. I'm sleeping."

"Well, wake up! I have an exclusive for you that The Register will be thanking you for, for years. They might even nominate you for a Pulitzer in Photojournalism."

"Can't stop pulling my chain, huh? And I'm just a guy trying to earn a decent living."

"Decent being the key word. Yes, my child! Come right up here on Santa's lap and tell him what you want for Christmas!"

Mike could not believe his ears. "Are you doing what I think you're doing?"

"Probably, Mike."

"Where?"

"At Lindsay's church." He gave him the address. "Make it fast and you'll get an exclusive photo essay about Dean Singleton Copley changing his image. You can run that tomorrow or the next day. Plus, the publicity for Lindsay's church might help them later on."

"I'll believe this when I see it," Mike muttered, pulling on his ski parka. His golden retriever nuzzled against his leg. "All right, Nikki.

You can come along for the ride. We'll see all about Dean Singleton Copley and 'exposure' for his new image."

It was nearly midnight before the last of the crowd went home. Lindsay looked around the parish hall and her heart warmed at all the smiling faces she saw.

"We never expected so many people." Mrs. Cabral said.

A murmur of approval spread through the room. From the back someone called: "You did a greaat job, Santa!"

Everyone burst into a spontaneous round of applause. Dean removed his artificial beard and stood to address his new friends.

"I can't thank you enough for making me feel so at home here. There's been such an outpouring of kindness towards me. I wish everyone could feel this good!"

"When will the pictures be in The Register?" Mrs. Cabral asked.

"Tomorrow morning's edition."

"Great publicity for the church, Dean."

"Can we get Mike back for the spaghetti supper?"

"Would you help us with the spring social?"

"Could you be a consultant for our finance board?"

Dean seemed pleased, turning from question to question. "No doubt."

He looked at Lindsay and her heart gave a lurch. The happiness in his eyes was an expression she would always remember.

*Thank you, Lord, for the happiness he has found. He's such a good man!*

And deep in her heart, she also thanked the good Lord for sending Dean and his family into her life.

"I can't believe how good everything smells." Melissa beamed at Meg and Lindsay in the cozy kitchen as they prepared their Thanksgiving meal. "Thank you for having me."

"We're thrilled you could join us. My mother loves you." Meg tightened the strings of her "Kiss the Chef" apron. "And we want you here with us."

"Taste this gravy," Lindsay held the spoon proudly for Meg who blew on it before she took a sip.

"Out of this world," she pronounced.

"I'm going to fold the napkins," Melissa said and went off into the dining room.

As soon as she was out of earshot Meg grabbed Lindsay's arm.

"Are you sure none of these Copleys will ridicule Mom? Or be talking about her behind our backs?"

Lindsay's heart went out to her sister. She hugged Meg tight. Some day she'd tell Meg how the Copleys had ridiculed her behind her back, and she had lived through it. "Oh Meg, please try not to worry so much. You're going to drive yourself crazy."

"I just always feel like I'm doing things *to* Mom, not *for* her."

"We have to have trust Meg, and faith. I know Daddy would say we are doing the right thing."

"I'll try to believe that..." Meg seemed unsure. "It's just so sad when you think we were all here together last Thanksgiving, and now this Thanksgiving everything's falling apart."

Lindsay felt the pain of this all too deeply. "I wish you didn't feel like that. Remember, 'to everything there is a season', Meg. 'There's a time for every purpose under Heaven.'" When would her sister let go and let God take over?

The doorbell chimed.

"Hello!" Mrs. Richardson called.

"I don't know if I should laugh or cry," Meg said.

Lindsay gave her shoulders an affectionate squeeze and went to answer the door. She found Dean, Mr. Copley and Claire smiling at her, holding platters, bags and a lovely floral arrangement. She realized that Mrs. Copely must have decided to go to Florida after all.

"Come in!"

"Belinda and Cassidy will be coming by later," Claire said.

"Oh good!" Lindsay was so happy to see them all, but it was the warmth in Dean's eyes that made her heartbeat quicken.

She said a silent prayer as she took their coats and bundles. *Thank you, Lord, for the gift of these dear new friends.* Imagine having these new folks in her life after the sad loss of her father. Although nothing could ever, ever replace him, their presence took away some of the sting and emptiness his death had brought.

They entered the warm kitchen and Lindsay introduced everyone around. She was so grateful that her mother was having a good day. She was relaxed and not frightened by all the activity. With

Alzheimer's patients, it was hard to predict which way things were going to go on any given day. Some days were easier than others.

"Mrs. Richardson, I'm so pleased to see you." Mr. Copley sat next to her and took her hand. "I am glad to be able to tell you how much I valued your husband's friendship, and what a fine man he was in every respect."

Mrs. Richardson smiled at him shyly.

"I remember you from the calling hours," Meg's voice was filled with appreciation.

"Your father and I didn't see each other too much of late, but the connection we shared was ever-strong."

Claire looked thoughtful. "That's the way it is sometimes."

The spirit moved Lindsay to take Meg's hand on one side of her, and Dean on the other. "We are so blessed to have each other," she said, her head lowered. In one motion, as if they were all of one mind and one heart, they all joined hands and offered a whispered "Amen."

Monday dawned bright and sunny and warm, as if it were a final gift of fall before the wintertime set in for good, even though the snow and ice they'd already had was a taste of things to come.

Lindsay's heart pounded furiously, and her palms felt damp. *Would her mother be all right? Would she resist placement in the home?*

*Lord, please let her have peace. Please.* Lindsay prayed with all her heart. Her mother had been through so much, she didn't want her frightened. At least they had shared a happy Thanskgiving. Those were memories she would always have to treasure.

She, Meg and her mother drove into the long, tree-lined drive at Greendale Glen around 11am.

"There's Aunt Charlotte's car," Lindsay said.

"Thank God for her," Meg said.

They pulled up to the grand entryway, with its portico and smooth, newly paved blacktop. French doors lined the manor house's front terrace, shaded by large chestnut and cypress trees.

Lindsay and Meg exchanged a look.

"I'll go in," Meg said.

Lindsay nodded, and scrambled up next to her mother in the front seat.

"How are you doing? Isn't this fun?" She patted her mother's knee.

But her mother just sat there, passive and listless.

Meg appeared with two attendants, a wheelchair, and a stylishly dressed professional looking woman who Lindsay took for the institution's Administrator.

The attendant opened the car door on the passenger side.

"Shall we take a look around, Mrs. Richardson?" His voice was gentle, he carefully helped move her from the car to the chair.

Mrs. Richardson didn't react at all, just sat complacently.

Lindsay could hardly believe her eyes. Her prayers had been answered. Her mother was showing no signs of fear, or anxiety, or disorientation. None of the trauma that Lindsay had feared was happening.

*Thank you, Dear Lord,* she thought. But it troubled her that her mother was like a rag doll.

She got out of the car, too, and followed them into Greendale Glen, Meg leading the way. Lindsay noted the charming holiday decorations and luxurious atmosphere of the entry foyer.

Three long wings stretched off from a central atrium. Residents and visitors strolled and chatted in a sunny, peaceful setting that opened up to a broad, exterior terrace. Lindsay imagined that the landscaped grounds were lovely in the summertime.

Aunt Charlotte approached and started helping to oversee the activity. After kissing Lindsay and Meg, and her sister, she turned her attention to directing the attendants.

Lindsay couldn't believe it: there were so many details to resolve. Nutritionists, physical therapists, the chaplain, pharmacists, housekeepers...the list seemed endless.

She walked quietly by her mother's side, holding her hand. It was warm soft, just as she always remembered it.

In her heart, she was saying good-bye.

They made their way down the plush carpeted hallway and for the first time, Lindsay noticed the institutional smell of the place. She sighed.

Just then, her cell phone rang.

"How's it going, Lindsay?" Dean's voice was full of caring and concern.

She gulped back the lump that was forming in her throat. "So far, it's a nursing home, but really, it's fine, Dean. My mother doesn't seem to mind at all. And everyone here is really nice."

"I know."

"What do you mean, you know?"

"I'm here, in the lobby, Lindsay. If that's okay. I brought something for your mother's room. It's one of those bed-in-a-bag sets, with those little purple flowers on it."

"Violets?" Her voice was husky with emotion.

"I guess so. Can I come down?"

Lindsay felt weak and shaky from the emotional upheaval of placement, and she was so touched that he cared enough to be there. Maybe it would do her mother good to see him, too.

"We're headed to her room now to get her settled. Then they're going to try and give her lunch."

"I'll be right there."

Dean met up with them shortly.

"Thanks for coming, Dean," Meg said.

"The comforter set is so pretty, Dean." Lindsay placed her hand on his arm. "Thank you."

"Let's go to the chapel for a minute," he suggested.

"I'll stay here," Meg said.

They entered the peaceful chapel and sat in one of the far pews.

"I can't imagine what this all feels like, Lindsay," he said.

Lindsay was thoughtful. "You know, I imagined when this moment came, and I thought it would be very sad. But it isn't that simple. There are a lot of emotions all at once."

"Like what?"

"Like nostalgia, for the old times. Like emptiness, for not having her to take care of in the house--or anywhere. Like resentment and fear, since I can't believe anyone else loves her enough to do a good job of taking care of her. Then there's doubt, grief, anxiety...and oddly enough, joy, too."

"Joy?" Dean seemed incredulous.

"Yes. Joy at the time God gave me with her. Joy for the memories, and the example of love. And joy for her, for having a new lease on life now. Maybe her appetite will come back here at Greendale Glen."

"I hope so."

"Me, too. We'll just have to wait and see. I hope Meg's okay, too, afterwards."

"I'm sure she will be okay. And I'm sure you will, too." Dean said.

Meg poked her head in and signaled to Lindsay. "It's time for us to go," she said, her voice full of resolve.

*Dear Lord, I trust you with it all,* Lindsay prayed to herself.

She and Dean rose and met Meg at the door. The sun streamed through the colorful stained-glass windows.

"I'm ready," Lindsay said.

Together, they all turned to face their futures.

# Chapter 15

"How do you like my office, Meg?" Lindsay put down her cup and saucer. Her heart warmed from the happy expression on her sister's face.

"It's beautiful, Lindsay, I'm very glad for you." Meg said. From the panorama of Lindsay's windows, a snowfall was gently decorating the scene along the picturesque riverbanks. "And I'm so proud of you. Just like Mom and Dad would be, too."

Lindsay squeezed her hand. "It hardly seems possible that three weeks have gone by."

"She's doing well there," Meg sounded upbeat.

"I don't know how you made it through exams and final grades and everything. The end of the semester is such a busy time for you."

Meg looked at her. "Frankly, I kept busy and I think that really helped take my mind off any negative feelings. Then look what happened! She's gained seven pounds since she's been there. So it looks like we did a good thing after all. And now it's almost Christmas Eve." She took Lindsay's hands in hers. "We're going to have to sell the house, you know."

Nodding, Lindsay was subdued in her reply. "I know. I've thought about that. It's the right time."

"I can't believe it, Lindsay. You're not upset. What a relief."

"It's okay, Meg. I knew it was coming."

With a decisive nod, Meg replied: "After the holidays we'll contact a realtor. You can always stay with me, you know."

Lindsay hopped up and gave her sister a hug. "Thank you, Meg. I do like it up here in the city. I'll look around up here and see what I can find."

"That's good," she nodded. "Are you sure you'll be all right while I'm in Florida?"

"The only thing wrong with me will be my extreme envy that I won't be in sunny Florida on semester break with you for two weeks, too." She held tight onto Meg's hands. "I want you to go and have a good time. Don't worry about Mom. I'll check in on her. You deserve to relax."

"Lindsay," Dean came in, holding his cell phone up to his ear.

"Dean! What's wrong?"

"Something's wacky at this skating rink in Newport we just finished. I have to go on site. It's a slush rink."

"Problems with the chiller system," Lindsay said.

"Right, I'll bet that's just what it is. Who was our mechanical contractor on that project?"

"I think it was the Bernardo Group."

"See if you can call them and have them meet us down there ASAP!"

He shifted his focus to Meg. "How you doing, Meg? Sorry to drag Lindsay away, but this is an emergency."

"I was just leaving, I'm meeting Jane at the Arcade," Meg answered, kissing Lindsay. "Good luck. See you at the house later."

Before she could leave, however, Mike and Claire came in to the office, both speaking at once.

"I told him to make an appointment, Dean --"

"You really ought to tell her I'm not a threat, Dean, especially since you just called me over."

Dean held up both hands and Claire and Mike fell silent.

"What power!" Meg exclaimed, causing everyone to laugh.

Eyeing Meg with interest, Mike extended his hand to her. "We haven't met yet. I'm Mike Malloy, staff photographer for The Register and a really good close personal friend of Dean's."

Raising an eyebrow, Dean quipped: "You are?"

"I'm Meg Richardson, Lindsay's sister."

"*Dr.* Meg Richardson," Lindsay interjected.

Meg and Mike shook hands..and suddenly the atmosphere in the room twinkled with pixie dust.

Dean and Lindsay exchanged a look.Claire's mouth dropped open.

Eventually, after what seemed to be a lifetime of starry-eyed gazing, Dean broke the spell. "You have your car, right, Mike?"

"Uh-huh." Mike didn't take his eyes off Meg.

"Why don't you follow us down to Newport?"

Claire excused herself, saying: "I have to set up the large conference room for later."

"And I need to hit the road, too." Meg reached into her oversized purse.

"I'll see you, Meg." Mike smiled debonairly. "If you're lucky."

Meg was the only one who found that funny. Dean and Lindsay exchanged a look while Meg was leaving.

"I'll meet you at the rink, Dean." Mike's tone seemed professional to Lindsay for the first time since he had entered the room.

"Good. Make sure you have a lot of film and that video camera, too."

As soon as he left, Lindsay grabbed Dean's arm and gasped: "What about that?"

Dean shrugged. "That's life. Might be good for both of them." They walked to his car. "We'll have lunch later, after I fix this crisis, okay?"

"Sure," she agreed.

They got into the Volvo and left the city behind. Before she knew it they had already zoomed across the Bay Side Bridge. "There's even more snow down here than at home," she remarked. The gray afternoon was thick and heavy through the seaside cloud cover. Festively decorated shops and homes had their lights turned on, bringing a real holiday feel to the air.

Newport looked like a fairy-tale village, with white lights twinkling in every store window, and street lamps wreathed in holly, tinsel and ornate decorations.

"It's so beautiful," breathed Lindsay.

They passed the impressive Tennis Hall of Fame on Bellevue Avenue and drove along the historic waterfront district. A huge Alaskan fir tree stood in the town square, colored lights dancing in the spunky sea breeze.

Lindsay opened her window and took a deep breath. "It smells like sea, pine and cooking. Divine!" she exclaimed.

"We'll have to send Meg and Mike down here," Dean said wryly. "Wouldn't that be something? They were certainly into each other."

"We'll have to keep our eyes on that situation. What do you think?" she asked.

"You never know," he answered.

They passed along the broad, tree-lined boulevard curving around on top of a bluff to offer a sweeping, magnificent view of the Atlantic Ocean. Waves crashed dramatically against the boulders on the shore, and crimson and gold clouds hung majestically as the sun poked through the slate-colored sky. He pulled over and parked the car.

"Let's sit here for a moment," he said.

"What about the rink?"

"The rink can wait." His eyes held hers. "Ever since I met you I'm seeing things I've never seen before, doing things I've never done before, appreciating life like I've never done before.

"I don't know how I can ever thank you, Lindsay. You've given me back my hope, and my promise, and my spirit. I wake up and I can't wait to get started. You've given me a new lease on life. I just wanted to tell you that. So you'll always know, no matter what happens."

"I'm so glad, Dean. But what do you mean, no matter what?"

He shrugged. "Well, you just never know what life has in store."

"That sounds too mysterious. I don't like it," Lindsay said. When he didn't answer, she continued. "But you're a great guy, and you deserve to have a happy, fulfilled life."

"There's only one way happiness will be mine now, Lindsay," Dean's voice sounded husky to her.

"Well, thank you for saying that, Dean. It was very nice of you." She smiled softly at him, and used her gentlest tone. "The holidays are an emotional time for lots of us." She did her best to come up with a kind reply. But deep inside, she couldn't help but wonder what he meant.

❧ ❧ ❧

"I still can't believe that you convinced my brother to dress up like Santa Claus."

Kathy's voice sounded smooth as molasses over the phone the following morning.

Lindsay absently flipped through a stack of mail waiting for her on her desk. How could she tell her that it had actually all been Dean's idea? That he was the one who volunteered after Salty threw his back out? Not that Dean wasn't a natural ham!

"You saw the pictures in The Register. They say 'a picture's worth a thousand words,' right?" Lindsay joked pleasantly.

She forced herself to stay focused, although her head was a million miles away. There were so many details to take care of with Christmas right around the corner. How had Dean convinced her to help with his open house the following night?

"He looked like he enjoyed it. I couldn't believe it." Kathy said.

"He did get a lot of pleasure out of making those kids so happy." Lindsay said. In her mind's eye, she saw him, smiling with Cassidy and Kodi. "He's so good with children."

"Who would have thought?" Kathy said with a laugh. She paused and Lindsay wondered what she was going to say next. Probably wanted something...but she tried to keep her thoughts charitable.

Finally, Kathy spoke. "You know, I've been thinking. It might not be a bad idea for us to get to know each other a little better. That scene in the office was just terrible."

Lindsay's stomach flipped. Or, more like it, turned. Did Kathy need another fashion disaster to ridicule? Or someone else to set up as an intruder? After the most recent disaster in the office, Lindsay didn't want to have any part of that.

And yet, she didn't want to refuse, either. Although Lindsay wasn't jumping at the chance, she decided to give it a try. After all, it was nearly Christmas Eve.

She swallowed. Hard. "Sounds nice, Kathy. You tell me when and where."

"How about if I come to the office tomorrow? Maybe I can even help out with that day-care project you and Gwynneth are working on."

"All right. But we really haven't done too much on it yet."

"That's fine," Kathy said agreeably.

When Lindsay hung up, she kept trying to convince herself that everything was normal, but something wasn't setting right with her. She tried to put her doubts aside.

*We'll let tomorrow take care of itself*, she thought. But those little seeds of suspicion in her heart were growing into big, huge blossoms of uncertainty faster than she could weed them out.

Lindsay dressed with special care in the morning. She chose a white cashmere turtleneck, black and white wool hound's tooth slacks, and black leather boots.

The morning went by quickly, with Lindsay and Claire going over resumes for the child-care positions they had received for the new day care center. Whenever it became a reality.

"Despite the feeling that we're not doing too much, we really are coming right along," Lindsay remarked as they went through the stack of applications they had received.

"It'll be open in May! That hardly seems possible." Claire was beaming. "I can get Cassidy started there right away."

There was a knock on the door to Lindsay's office. Lindsay and Claire looked at each other and mouthed: "Dean."

"Come on in," she called..

"Patience," Claire said.

With a smile, Lindsay asked: "Who, Claire? You or me?"

In walked Dean, his eyes wide with excitement. "Lindsay! I wrote up--" He stopped when he saw her. "Are you going out?"

She shook her head in response.

"Well, it's just that you look like you're dressed up."

"Lindsay always looks nice, Dean," Claire prompted.

He frowned. "I know, Claire." Looking at Lindsay, he added: "Rule number two: never work with a close personal friend."

"Too late, and you're repeating yourself," Lindsay said. They all laughed.

After a moment Claire spoke. "Did you have a question, Dean? Because Lindsay and I are selecting some candidates to interview."

"Good. Maybe we'll get that thing open some time before all these kids are out of high school. Why don't you show me those resumes now?" He left as quickly as he had arrived.

"I wonder what's with him?" Lindsay scooped up the papers and rolled her eyes. "I won't let him tell us who to hire, Claire. We'll get who we want."

"See how he trusts you, though?"

With a smile, Lindsay nodded. "Are you coming to the open house tonight?"

"I'll be there. Let me know if I can help."

Patting Claire's shoulder, Lindsay replied: "Thank you. Just be there and have a good time. And bring B and C," Lindsay used the nicknames she had dubbed for Belinda and Cassidy.

"I will. It will be so nice when Shane gets back from active duty. Belinda and all of us miss him so much. And Cassidy is growing so fast."

"Christmas doesn't feel right when someone is gone, does it?" Lindsay was thoughtful. Her first Christmas without her father, and with her mother no longer at home, brought the reality of that close to her. "Shane will be here soon and next Christmas for sure, Claire, I just know it."

On the way to Dean's office, Lindsay pondered the changes in her life since last year. Back then, she didn't even know Dean. And now...he meant more to her than she liked to think about.

"Dean?" she tapped on his door.

"Yup, come in." he answered.

"I brought these in, to start, Dean. But I haven't finished looking at all the-"

"Where are you really going?" His eyes flashed.

"What?"

"I think you're going out."

Lindsay couldn't believe her ears. "Dean Singleton Copley, you're jealous."

"No, I'm not." His voice was rich with expression.

"You are!"

"I just don't want you blabbing company business to anyone."

Lindsay smiled. "Come on. Don't you think I'm professional enough to know what's not appropriate to discuss?"

"I didn't mean that."

"Okay then. What did you mean, though?"

When Dean didn't answer, she took a wild guess. "I'm not meeting Mike Malloy, if that's what you mean. He likes Meg, remember?"

"Well, then who?"

So she was right. He was jealous.

"Dean, your sister Kathy called me and I'm meeting her here."

"Kathy? Listen, Lindsay. Do you really think that's a good idea?"

She shrugged. "Well, it's not an idea I'd come up with. But when she called me and asked if she could stop by today I didn't want to say no. On Christmas Eve, too, Dean."

He gave her a look. "Why do you think Kathy wants to see you?"

"She said to smooth things over."

"I don't think it's a good idea."

Glancing at her watch, she winced. "It's getting late. I appreciate your interest, but she'll be here soon."

"Well, just cancel it. Say something came up and stay here."

"No. I said I'd meet her here, Dean, and I will. It will be okay."

"I just don't want to see you get hurt."

"What do you mean?"

"Why do you think she wants to see you? Do you really believe that she wants to be friends?"

"I haven't thought so far ahead, to tell you the truth."

He eyed her. "You should. Maybe you're a little too trusting, don't you think? I'd be suspicious of her if I were you."

Lindsay felt the blood rush to her face as she remembered the scene in the powder room at the Club. "I'll keep that in mind, Dean. You may very well have a point. But I'm hoping she's on the up and up."

As she left his office, she heard him calling: "Tell me when you're done, okay?"

She smiled and waved okay over her shoulder. "Wish me luck, Dean."

*Let me be an instrument of your peace, Lord*, she prayed as she tucked her unruly curls into a neat bun at the base of her neck on her way back to her office. *Where there is hatred, let me sow love.* The Beatitudes were one of her favorite passages.

And although her feelings had been deeply hurt by Kathy's previous hypocrisy, it was very possible the olive branch she was offering now was sincere. Her instincts told her it wasn't the case, but she vowed to keep an open mind.

Yet Dean's comments might have some credence. He knew Kathy better than she did. When she arrived at her office, Claire gave her a funny look. But: "She's in there," is all she said.

Lindsay went in, only to find Mrs. Copley standing there. "How nice to see you, Mrs. Copley."

"Hello, Lindsay. I was visiting Mr. Copley here and I wanted to see if your church would have any use for these." She indicated a beautifully decorated gift basket on the table. "There's a few gift certificates to a day of beauty treatments at the Élan Spa."

A quick glance in the basket told Lindsay it held dozens of envelopes!

"How thoughtful! I don't know if you knew, but we're having an Attic Treasures Afternoon in January, and this would be the perfect kind of gift! It's wonderful. Thank you, Mrs. Copley."

A smile crossed Mrs. Copley's lips. And unlike before, this time there was true feeling in her eyes.

"Would you be able to stay for some coffee, or tea, with me?"

"No, no," Mrs. Copley waved her hands. "I have to get to another appointment. I only stopped in to see how Dean's father was feeling being back in the office."

Lindsay wasn't sure, but she thought that Mrs. Copley seemed a bit shy. "I wish you could visit a while," she said. "Maybe another time?"

Mrs. Copley nodded and crossed the office to the door. "That would be lovely."

"Merry Christmas, then, Mrs. Copley."

"And Merry Christmas to you, too, Lindsay dear." She placed her hand briefly on top of Lindsay's at the doorknob. It was a warm and motherly gesture.

"Thank you again. And please come back soon!"

Off she swept, all furs and perfume and jewels...but this time, there was a little something else. The lightness in her step warmed Lindsay's heart. Mrs. Copley seemed happy.

"Wasn't that something?" she asked Claire.

"Like I said, they're great people. Even the one waiting for you in Dean's office now. Just that some growing up needs to be done there."

"Thanks, Claire. But why is she in Dean's office?"

Claire just shrugged.

Lindsay went down the hall and found the door to Dean's office open. Kathy and Gwynneth were sitting together, sharing a laugh over an open scrapbook filled with old photographs. When they saw Lindsay, they fell silent.

"Am I early?" she asked.

"No, no. Gwynneth and I were just reminiscing about some of the good old days. All of Dean's old girlfriends. Before you came along."

Lindsay felt as if the floor could swallow her up. "Where is Dean, anyway?"

"He had to go over to the Engineering Department." Gywnneth spoke quickly.

Lindsay nodded. Should she ask Gwynneth to come along to her office to review the plans? But her question was answered for her almost instantly.

"And remember Bailey Pembroke?" Kathy asked. She and Gwynneth burst out laughing.

Lindsay wondered if she were being tested.She felt like she was back in high school, a goofball girl looking in on the cliquey cool girls. "What about the plans?"

"Why don't we stop by my office and see that fabric swatch for the new drapes?" Gwynneth asked.

Kathy turned from Gwynneth to Lindsay. "Would you mind waiting one minute?"

Lindsay realized then there would be no meeting. They would not be looking at the plans. And there would be no friendship with Kathy. Oh well. She didn't fit into that world, anyway.

"No problem." Lindsay agreed.

"I'll just put this here," Kathy went to place her teacup on Dean's desk and lost her balance, spilling her beverage on his desk.

"Oh no!"

"I'll get some towels." Gwynneth scurried out of the room.

"Let me tell Claire." Kathy ran out behind her before Lindsay could say anything.

Dashing over to the wet bar, Lindsay grabbed a stack of paper towels and began blotting. "I wonder if clumsiness is contagious?" she said out loud.

With shaking hands, she took the scrapbook over to the sofa and began looking at it.

Fifteen minutes later, she knew what she had to do. She placed the scrapbook back on Dean's desk and blotted her eyes as she walked from the office to see Claire.

"You look like you've seen a ghost!" her friend exclaimed.

"I think I have," she mumbled. "Where's Dean, Claire? I need to see him right away. And can you please make me an appointment to see Mr. Copley ASAP?"

"Sure," Claire called as Lindsay drifted into her office.

She passed Gwynneth's on the way and found the two friends still engaged in a lively social visit.

"I'll be in my office if you want to see me. Come by and we'll go over the plans, then maybe we'll get a coffee." Or not. The meaning of what she had just seen was numbing her to anything else. She didn't even hear Kathy's reply.

# Chapter 16

Dean knew he needed to clear his mind and let the car take him...wherever. Before he knew it, he found himself in the sleepy suburb where Lindsay had lived with her mother and Meg, a light snowfall gently dusting the charming tree-lined streets. The reflective tunes of Jim Brickman's piano filtering from his CD player seemed to match his mindset perfectly.

His time with Lindsay this past month had been so enjoyable, more than he had expected. What kind of woman would be able to joke around, laugh, and enjoy a hearty Italian meal under such extenuating circumstances? Only one that was very, very special. Only one like Lindsay.

Images of her kind smile flashed through his mind.

Her tousled curls, frank, honest gaze, the soft curve of her cheek...all of this and a deep faith, too. A woman who was contemporary, yet traditional. Lindsay Richardson seemed to have it all.

And that was just the problem, he mused as he coasted along the on-ramp back to the highway. Lindsay was living a pretty full life, and from what he could tell, a quite fulfilling one, without him. The lights of Providence twinkled in the distance, the volume of traffic much heavier since he had left the sleepy suburbs behind. Skillfully, confidently, he moved through the congestion and turned on to the East Side exit.

Thirty-two and single. Not the kind of life he'd have designed for himself. Seems that the Lord had other plans for him like the family business. Only that route was not the one he'd have chosen for himself.

He called into his mailbox at work.

"You have nine new messages," the computerized voice reported.

Dean scrolled through them, making mental notes of which ones needed urgent replies and which ones could wait. An employee with a broken-down company vehicle in South County, twenty-three miles away. A late delivery on two condensing units. A single mother office worker with a three-year old, calling from the emergency room at Rhode Island Hospital.

His mother.

His mother. It was beyond him why they didn't see the reason for his being a compulsive workaholic. Guilt had a way of doing that to you.

Dean pictured his mother at her escritoire in her ornate, cavernous marble and gilt-worked writing room, with the satin salmon wall covering imported from Italy.

Contrast her cold scene with the cozy warmth of the Richardson's modest kitchen. Dean remembered the affection and sincerity of the little Barringtown ranch house. In his whole life, he had never been a part of such a warm and natural family scene. Until he met Lindsay and she opened her world and her heart to him, he had only wondered what it would feel like. When he thought of the differences, it was a stark and biting comparison. No wonder Lindsay looked askance at his materialistic existence. He couldn't blame her in the least.

He sighed. The final message in his mailbox was from one of his insulation contractors, refusing to show up at their next installation because the correct equipment he needed hadn't arrived yet. He would have to deal with them later.

Pulling into his driveway, he pushed the button for his automatic garage door opener.

Sometimes, just sometimes, Dean wondered if running Copley Industries was really the thing for him. And all of a sudden, since he met Lindsay a month ago, he didn't feel so alone in his musings when his thoughts took this path.

Her words echoed in his mind: "You do have a right to be happy, Dean. God wants it for you. And I just know that your father does, too."

Normally he knew right away which way to go with his life. In all aspects of his life, Dean Singleton Copley was usually the one to call the shots.

And now that was all turned upside down. Not only was he realizing his deep and growing feelings for her, not only was he understanding that a higher power was the one that was ultimately directing his life, but he also knew that his character was the way it was and that there was no going back. He closed the garage door behind him, knowing his mind was made up. And feeling at peace about all of it. Hopefully Lindsay would see things his way.

For some reason Lindsay couldn't get in touch with Dean before her four p.m. appointment with his father. She smoothed her tousled curls and mustered up her courage. Just as she had done a month earlier, she gripped the handle of her father's briefcase for courage. But unlike before, this time Lindsay knew it wasn't going to be easy. There was something ironic about the cheery holiday decorations and blinking colored lights all around her.

She knocked purposefully on the elder Mr. Copley's door, the right door this time. To her surprise, she found it ajar.

"Come in, Lindsay, I was expecting you. How are you?" Mr. Copley greeted her warmly. Holding the door open with one hand, he took her arm with the other. "What can I do for you?"

His eyes looked so warm and sincere. This was a man at peace. Lindsay felt so glad to see him looking so good, but at the same time needed his blessing.

"I'm fine, thank you," she answered as he led her to a sofa along the wall.

He handed her a crystal tumbler filled with sparkling mineral water. A fresh lemon wedge bobbed happily amid the bubbles and ice cubes. Her mind went back to their welcome home get-together; it was not so long ago, and yet, to Lindsay, it seemed like a lifetime had passed since then.

"You are always so thoughtful," she said with a smile, truly touched by Mr. Copley's attentiveness.

"Thank you." He sat beside her, looking at her with a fond, nostalgic smile. "Sometimes the resemblance to your dad is so clear." He shook his head.

"You've been so good to me, Mr. Copley." Her voice was quivering with emotion.

His brows drew together in a puzzled frown. "This sounds like an uh-oh," he said warily.

She nodded. "I'm afraid you're right." Placing her tumbler on the smoked glass and copper coffee table before her, she faced him. "I so appreciate your generosity in hiring me, and having me here. And I've been so very happy."

"But..."

She moistened her lips. "But I can't stay."

His blue eyes, so much like Dean's that it pained her to look at him, widened in surprise.

"Why not, dear? Are you ill?"

She shook her head, emotions welling up. Tears filled her eyes and threatened to spill over on to her best black sweater. "Not physically, anyway. But I am heartsick."

He tilted his head to one side and looked at her quizzically. "Go on," he urged.

"Your son is a great guy in many ways, Mr. Copley. He really is. And as I've worked here, I've gotten to know him better. And to understand him a little, too. I think. He's grown comfortable enough with me to tell me about himself. What he is really looking for in life. His higher purpose, if you will."

"Really?" Mr. Copley looked interested. "And?"

Lindsay took a sip of her water, before she found the courage to keep talking.

Mr. Copley spoke. "Well?"

She squared her shoulders. "I've fallen for him. Big time."

After a pause, Mr. Copley gave her a half-smile. "My dear, I want you to be happy. Shouldn't you be telling Dean this?"

"I am. But you gave me my chance here. I don't want to let you down."

She rose from the sofa and walked over to the plate glass windows. A light snowfall was dusting the city. Gazing out on the charming winter landscape before her, she took a deep breath.

"My father told me to follow my heart, and that I had a right to be happy in this world."

Mr. Copley's eyes seemed to warm. "Do you doubt that, Lindsay?"

Lindsay tried to calm down. "I do, now. Because I don't know where it will lead me. And I don't know what to do. That's why I wanted to talk to you. To ask your advice."

"Yes, I'm glad you did, my dear." He was holding her hands.

"I don't think I can stay." Her voice was sad.

He shook his head. "I'm not so sure."

Lindsay shook her head. "I wanted to tell you why I'm resigning. You've been so good to me. Thank you." She gathered her coat and her briefcase. "I'm sorry," she said as she moved toward the door.

"Where are you going now, dear?"

She shrugged. "Home, I guess." Even though it would be so empty and cold.

The silence hung heavily between them.

"You don't have to go," he said softly, his eyes filled with pain. Then something in them hardened. "Where is your courage? Would your father want you to run away and let me down? Worse, let yourself down?"

"I can't stay," she said, "I'm sorry." Her eyes searched his face. "I love him so much."

"Then you have to tell him. You do not have the right to throw your job away. Some might find you ungrateful."

"I'm not -"

Just then the copper doors opened and Dean appeared.

"Dad? I need to talk to you." He stopped in his tracks. "Lindsay! What are you doing here?"

Lindsay and Mr. Copley spoke at the same time.

"I was just leaving."

"She was speaking with me."

Dean looked back and forth between them carefully, then fixed his gaze on her. "You're crying, Lindsay? Why? Is it your mother?"

Lindsay couldn't contain herself.

"No, it's not my mother, Dean. It's you."

Dean looked puzzled, but he didn't say anything.

Her eyes brimming with tears, she fumbled her way over to the door.

"I have to get going." She found her way to the corridor.

Dean and his father stood side-by-side after she left, the elder man's arm on the other's shoulder.

"Go after her, son," he advised. His voice was gentle, yet firm. "She loves you."

# Chapter 17

Dean raced down the dimly lit corridor after Lindsay. The path towards her seemed to mirror his life since he had met her, his journey from the darkness to the light, with her at the end. He couldn't lose her now.

"Lindsay! Lindsay, wait!" he called.

She paused, not turning to face him.

Neither one of them saw the two well-coiffed heads poke out of Gwynneth's office, only to quickly disappear.

"Talk to me!" he called, this time even louder.

He caught up to her and took her by the arm, turning her to face him.

"I can't talk right now, Dean." She moved away from him, hoping he would not see her tearstained face.

"Why not, Lindsay?"

Her lower lip trembled. "I saw the photos."

Puzzled, he shook his head.

"The pictures of you and Bailey Pembroke. I'm sorry, I was with Kathy and she spilled coffee on your scrapbook."

"I can explain it. That's my scrapbook, with pictures of me and Ronald's fiancee. What about it?"

"Well, it bothers me, Dean..."

"Why?"

She sighed. "Because of how I feel for you. I love you so much, and it's scaring me."

Dean took her in his arms and with his free hand placed a finger over her lips in a gesture of "Ssssh". Then he motioned to Gwynneth's door.

"The truth is, Lindsay, that girl was Ronald's fiancee, and I never, ever put that scrapbook out," he murmured in a voice so low only she alone could hear it.

How obvious! Lindsay's eyes widened as she realized she had fallen for their set up. She nodded to him, letting him know she understood and would play along with his charade.

"Let me see if she's in here. Gwynneth!" Dean rapped on the door.

Instantly, Gwynneth appeared. "I'm here."

"Gwynneth." That was all he said.

Her face reddened and she receded into the dimly lit office.

Dean went in after her, with Lindsay following closely behind.

"Talk," he commanded to Kathy and Gwynneth. "Just spill it."

It didn't take long.

"Don't blame me, it was all her idea." Gwynneth pointed to Kathy.

"You can't blame me, Dean. I did it for all of us." Kathy said heatedly.

As if he knew it would continue back and forth until the cows came home, Dean held up his hands in a gesture of 'halt'. He eyed the two with distaste. "It was your idea, Kathy?"

With a sigh, and a sideways glance at Lindsay, Kathy admitted: "Yes."

"I wasn't really a part of things," Gwynneth said.

"You know, you're not very attractive when you squirm, ladies," Dean said.

"How can you be like this to me?" As Gwynneth spoke, Lindsay found herself actually feeling sorry for her.

"And I suppose I should apologize?" Kathy continued. "Well, I'm not going to. It was just a prank."

"Maybe you could just explain where you're coming from, then, Kathy?" Lindsay probed gently.

Gwynneth scoffed. "Yeah. Let's analyze a joke to death."

Kathy looked from Dean to Lindsay, then back again. But she remained quiet.

"Tell her about it," Gwynneth continued. "It's all going to come out, anyway! Or do you want me to tell them, Kat?" Gwynneth persisted.

"All right, all right." Kathy looked at Dean. "Derek is having terrible financial problems, Dean. I was just fooling around with Lindsay to take my mind off it."

Chewing her lower lip vigorously, Kathy continued: "We're ruined. Totally. To put it in a nutshell." She clenched her teeth. "Only because of the stock market. And his gambling problem."

"So this practical joke about Bailey..."

"Then it would help me forget the story about Derek's whole family being ruined. I'm sorry, Lindsay." She turned to face Lindsay. "You don't deserve this. You're not really a part of our lives."

"She is now, Kathy." Dean's voice broke the awkward silence in the room.

"What do you mean, Dean?" Kathy's eyes bugged out.

Gwynneth gasped, clasping both hands over her mouth. "No!"

"Just what I said," he answered.

"I told you, Kathy! There's nothing left for me here." Gwynneth grabbed her coat and purse. "I'm history."

"Please," Lindsay said. "Don't overreact. Try not to be angry."

Her heart was heavy at the thought of how disappointed Gwynneth must have been to realize that Dean would never be hers.

"No one could ever tell you what to do, Dean. Ever." Kathy held the door for Gwynneth. "It's your life, after all. I guess it all comes down to that."

Gwynneth paused, placing her hand on her forehead.

"Maybe some day I'll be able to say I'm sorry I was so rotten to you, Lindsay. But it's not going to happen today."

Lindsay eyed her steadily. "Take care, Gwynneth."

"Right. You, too." Gwynneth murmured as she left.

Kathy slammed the door. "What a touching scene." She held her chin up, high and proud, looking every bit to the core the Copley that she was. But knowing the family a little, Lindsay detected an apprehension in her, behind the brittle mask she wore.

"Kathy," Dean's voice was gentle. "We are family."

Her shoulders drooped and she looked at Dean. "I'm so confused..."

"It's all right." He took he in his arms for a long moment, just holding her and stroking her hair.

"I missed you," he said.

She gave a ladylike sniffle. "Oh, me too, Dean." She wiped her eyes.

Dean produced a handkerchief, saying: "I'm going to investigate stock options in this area of men's accessories. Handkerchiefs will be a gold mine for us." His tone was wry.

"I'm so sorry. And Lindsay." Kathy turned to face her. "Try not to be too hard on me."

Lindsay touched her arm lightly. "It's okay, Kathy," she said gently.

"No, it's not. I've been wretched to you."

"It'll be okay, Kathy," Dean added. "We'll sort out Derek's problems."

Kathy shook her head. "I didn't mean to make you look bad Dean. I'm sorry," she repeated.

"Forget it, Kathy. Are you still coming to the open house?"

"If you'll still have me."

Dean gave her shoulders a squeeze. "Of course."

"I'll see you there, then." Kathy took her briefcase and designer coat. "Lindsay, maybe we really can get that day care center going."

"I'd like to," Lindsay agreed.

"Are you sure you're all right? To drive and everything?"

"I'm fine, Dean. See you both later." She gave his cheek a quick peck. "I'm sorry," she whispered.

After she left, Dean leaned up against the desk, arms folded against his chest.

"And now it's just us."

She crossed the carpet, closing the distance between them.

"I like the sound of that," she said with a smile.

He took her hands. "Lindsay, I don't ever want to feel again the way I felt when you left Dad's office. It was like something in me died. I don't think I could bear it."

"I didn't like it, either. But I couldn't bear to think I would be working with you and still so in love with you."

Then, in one motion, Dean drew her close. Her heart rejoiced as they kissed, because the circle of his arms warmed her and filled her with the light of God's love.

# *Epilogue*

Dean was amazed at the turnout. Not only had his neighbors shown up, in complete holiday spirits, but his family, as well.

He looked around his living room, aglow with holiday lights, and warmed with holiday spirit, and for a moment, felt like the luckiest man in the whole world.

"Dean, would you like me to freshen up the punch?"

Looking at Claire's smiling face, and Cassidy's chubby cheeks shining in the Christmas warmth, Dean nearly melted with affection and appreciation.

"If you let me hold Cassidy," he answered.

Claire transferred the baby easily to Dean's waiting arms. The baby patted at his smiling face, playfully contented at being in his charge.

"It's a real success, Dean."

He turned to Lindsay, his heartbeat quickening at the sight of her. Flushed with winter warmth and glowing with Christmas cheer, Lindsay appeared to him to be the epitome of womanly beauty.

"Hi, Lindsay." Did that sound as lame to her as he felt it had been?

"Oh, hi, Dean. Merry Christmas!" Lindsay hugged him impulsively. "That's for my mother and Meg, too."

"They're coming, aren't they?"

"I think so. They're planning on it. But we'll have to see." In her heart of hearts, Lindsay was sure they'd be able to make this party. It was so special to her, in so many ways. The Copleys had become more than friends to her lately; they had shared so much that they were coming very close to what 'family' really meant.

"Lindsay."

Dean's voice brought her back into the moment. When she heard him speak, the cheery chatter of the invited guests just muted into the background. It was as if Dean's voice was all she needed to hear.

"I know we're in the kitchen," he continued, "and I've got a baby balanced on my hip, but if you'd help me for a minute?"

"Sure!"

He struggled to extract the box from his pocket.

"There's something I wanted to show you."

He held up the box, an emerald green velvet treasure, so promising in its very presence.

Lindsay looked at him, her eyes filled with wonder.

"You know me, Lindsay. Almost better than I know myself. And there's only one way I can be happy. And whole."

"Ooh," she breathed. Could this be what she thought? Now?

"I told you in Newport, 'no matter what', remember? No matter what happens, I have to be with you, whatever life has in store." He bent on one knee to the tile floor, still cradling Cassidy, who snuggled comfortably in his warm, protective arms.

"And what I meant by that, Lindsay Richardson, is that I love you. You've shown me what it means to love, and how it feels to be loved. I can't ever thank you enough. But I love you, and tonight, I offer you my heart, now and forever, no matter what. Let's see what life has in store for us together. If you'll have me."

Tears filled Lindsay's eyes, tears of joy, and fulfillment, and profound gratitude at the awesome, glorious wonder of God's loving presence in their lives. For in her heart, she knew it was His redeeming grace, and the Holy Spirit, that was guiding them along such a joyous and fulfilling path.

"Will you marry me?"

"Yes, Dean!" She embraced him, raising him up in a gesture of everlasting love. "I will marry you!"

Cassidy gurgled in delight, clapping her hands and squealing at the top of her lungs. Lindsay opened the shutters over the pass-through counter, revealing the kitchen to the living room and dining room area. Cassidy's laughter captured the attention of the partygoers, who turned towards them in curiosity.

"I guess we'd better tell them," Dean said.

Just then Meg and Mrs. Richardson joined the festivities, smiling and very much at ease. Lindsay was overjoyed at the sight of them, and exclaimed, "Oh, yes, go ahead, tell them, Dean!"

He stood at full height and smiled, his countenance as bright and as radiant as the sun on Easter morning. "At last," he said in a voice only meant for Lindsay, "I have finally made the perfect proposal!"

The End

If you enjoyed this author's book, then please place a review up at the site of purchase, and any social media sites you frequent!

You can find ALL our books up on our website at:

*https://www.writers-exchange.com*

All Regina's Books:

*https://www.writers-exchange.com/Regina-Andrews/*

All our romances:

*https://www.writers-exchange.com/category/genres/romance/*

https://dl.bookfunnel.com/cwmeub2oxo

# *About the Author*

A resident of Providence, R.I., Regina grew up in the nearby suburb of Barrington. After graduating from Providence College she attended the University of Delaware, and eventually returned to Providence to earn her Master's Degree in American Civilization from Brown University. She is inspired by the natural world and she and her husband enjoy visiting nearby Cape Cod, M.A. Some of her other hobbies include travel, museums, theater, classical music, coral singing, gardening, and anything French. In her spare time, she is a radio host for In-Sight Radio, a national association for the visually impaired of all ages.

For more on Regina's body of work, visit:

http://www.ReginaAndrews.com

For all of Regina's Writers Exchange books, go to her author page:

https://www.writers-exchange.com/Regina-Andrews/

*If you want to read more about other books by this author,*

*they are listed on the following pages...*

# Spotlight on Love

When duty calls, can love survive the battlefield?

Providence, 1941. Nurse Helen Middleton has sacrificed everything--her music, her youth, her dreams--to support her family during hard times. But when charismatic Postmaster William "Red" Williamson sweeps into her life with flowers, charm, and encouragement, Helen begins to imagine a future filled with song and love.

Then Pearl Harbor shatters the nation's innocence, and Helen's world turns upside down. Red is pulled into a dangerous covert mission overseas, while Helen enlists as an Army nurse and is deployed to war-torn North Africa. As espionage, betrayal, and tragedy close in, Helen must summon every ounce of courage to save the man she loves--and prove that even in the darkest times, love can light the way.

Fans of inspirational romance, wartime suspense, and strong heroines will be swept away by *Spotlight on Love*--a story of sacrifice, resilience, and the enduring power of the human heart.

Publisher: https://www.writers-exchange.com/spotlight-on-love/

# Sterling Lakes Series

## {Inspirational Romance}

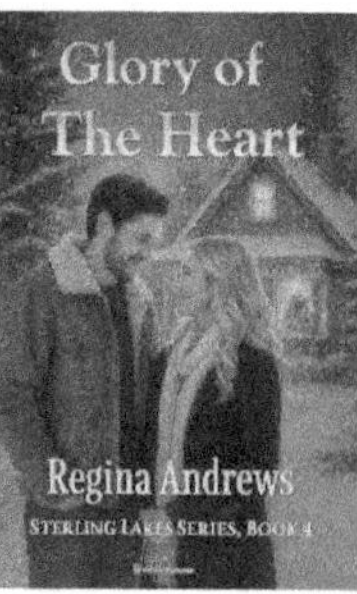

*Sterling Lakes is more than just a small New England town--it's a place where the past and present meet, where wounds run deep but faith runs deeper, and where God's light shines through the cracks of even the most broken hearts.*

*From a stained-glass artist haunted by childhood scars, to a journalist fighting to preserve history, a shy librarian learning to step into the light, and a war hero searching for hope after loss-- the residents of Sterling Lakes discover that renewal begins within.*

*Each story in Regina Andrews' Sterling Lakes Series celebrates the courage to forgive, the beauty of second chances, and the glory of love that transforms lives. Against the backdrop of a town rediscovering its spirit, four romances intertwine to reveal a single truth: no matter the past, God's light can restore every heart.*

**LIGHT OF THE HEART,** Book 1: Cascade Preston swore she'd never return to Sterling Lakes.

The memories are too dark, the wounds too deep. But when a church renovation calls for her stained-glass artistry, Cascade finds herself face-to-face with both her past--and the determined project manager, Dan McQuay.

Dan refuses to take no for an answer. His steady presence and quiet faith begin to crack Cascade's protective shell. Yet opening her heart means risking the pain she's carried for years.

As the church rises from neglect, Cascade must decide: will she keep running from the town she associates with silence, or embrace forgiveness and the possibility of love?

Light of the Heart is a moving Inspirational Romance about second chances, healing from the past, and finding hope where you least expect it.

Publisher: https://www.writers-exchange.com/light-of-the-heart/

**ANGELS OF THE HEART**, Book 2: Maryanne Lynch thrives on her career as a television journalist in Sterling Lakes. But nothing prepares her for the shock of developer Travis Collimore's plan to demolish the historic Townsend Barn--a landmark Maryanne treasures as part of the town's heart.

Determined to save the barn, Maryanne throws herself into the fight. But the more she opposes Travis, the more she glimpses the man beneath the title--a man whose quiet conviction stirs feelings she never expected.

With the town divided, Maryanne must decide if her heart belongs to the past she's protecting, or the future she might build with Travis.

Angels of the Heart is a heartfelt Inspirational Romance about trust, forgiveness, and love that can rise from even the fiercest of conflicts.

Publisher: https://www.writers-exchange.com/angels-of-the-heart/

**PRAISE OF THE HEART,** Book 3: Laura Matthewson has always kept to herself. As Sterling Lakes' librarian, she finds comfort among books, not people--especially when all eyes are on the town's returning hero, baseball star Cliff Markham.

Cliff came home to help raise funds for St. Luke's Church, but he didn't expect to be drawn to the shy librarian who avoids the spotlight. Laura's gentle spirit captivates him, yet she struggles to believe she belongs in his world.

As the fundraiser heats up, Laura must face her fears and decide whether to keep hiding in the shadows--or step into the light of love and faith.

Praise of the Heart is a tender Inspirational Romance about courage, community, and discovering the strength God placed within you.

Publisher: https://www.writers-exchange.com/praise-of-the-heart/

**GLORY OF THE HEART,** Book 4: CC Cogshell came to Sterling Lakes for a fresh start. A former detective with a broken heart, she's determined to rebuild her life on her own terms. The last thing she expects is Perrin Stafford--a decorated war hero and sculptor--showing up on her doorstep just before Christmas.

For Perrin, returning to his childhood home stirs bittersweet memories. Grieving his late wife and burdened by secrets from his father's past, he's unsure whether faith--or love--has a place in his future.

Drawn together by chance, CC and Perrin discover that healing sometimes comes in unexpected ways. Between attic discoveries, holiday traditions, and the glow of a church reborn, they must decide if they're willing to let go of the past and embrace the glory God offers in the present.

Glory of the Heart is a moving Inspirational Romance about second chances, faith restored, and love that shines brightest in the darkest seasons.

Publisher: https://www.writers-exchange.com/glory-of-the-heart/

# The Perfect Proposal

Lindsay Richardson never expected her new job at Copley Industries to change her life. One chance interview with the elder Mr. Copley lands her a position she desperately needs—but also puts her face-to-face with his son, Dean Singleton Copley, the commanding executive who allows no room for mistakes.

To Dean, business comes first, last, and always. But Lindsay's resilience and warmth prove difficult to ignore. As deadlines mount and Boston glitters with Christmas lights, she challenges Dean to see beyond contracts and control.

Between family traditions, church gatherings, and the quiet hope of the season, love begins to grow in unexpected places.

Can the holidays soften Dean's guarded heart, or will fear and pride keep him from making the perfect proposal?

A warm and wholesome holiday romance, *The Perfect Proposal* is perfect for readers who love Christmas settings, clean romance, and happily-ever-afters.

Publisher: https://www.writers-exchange.com/the-perfect-proposal/

**If you want to read more about other Romance novels by this publisher, they are listed on...**

https://www.writers-exchange.com/category/genres/romance/

**You can find ALL our books on our website at:**
https://www.writers-exchange.com

**All Regina's Books:**
https://www.writers-exchange.com/Regina-Andrews/